Here I Am

STORIES BY
Boo Hansen

Shadow Press

ISBN 978-0615957135

Printed in the United States of America

CONTENTS

POSTMORTEM

I STAND BEHIND COUNSEL TABLE making my argument. The judge appears to be dozing. My client, Henry Burks, sits beside me looking worried, as well he should. Technically, my client is a corporation, and Henry is merely its current president, here to put a human face on the company-without-conscience he represents. It is not a pretty face – droopy and large of pore – but it is remarkably similar to the one behind the bench. White. Old. Male. So that helps.

At least Henry won't go to jail. This is a civil suit, so the only issue is money. The company can afford to lose this one – a distinct possibility if a fair-minded jury ever hears the unfortunate facts – but it's my task to keep that from happening. I'm urging the judge to dismiss the case in its infancy, based on a strong if unappealing point of law. What a layman might term a "technicality" but I prefer to call a godsend.

As usual, my desire to win is tinged in desperation. Losing at trial is ignominious enough, but my firm compounds the humiliation by conducting a postmortem after every trial that is lost. During this sadistic ritual, the legal strategies are dissected, the misjudgments microscopically examined, and the war stories embalmed for posterity. Even those lawyers pilloried in the past show no mercy. Especially those lawyers, come to think of it. Preparation, I've learned, is the key to winning. And I am thoroughly prepared for this oral argument. So it is unsettling, to say the least, when my brain blows a fuse and goes dark.

I am mid-way through a sentence when I stop talking. My jaw is frozen open and my mind is a blank. A murky thought finally emerges like weak headlights through the fog. Something is vaguely, terribly wrong. I have the strange sensation that I've lost time; the court reporter's tapping fingers now lay listless in her lap. The silence builds, becomes more insistent, until finally it rouses the judge. Beside me, Henry clears his throat and squirms in his chair. But I'm still stumped. I have absolutely no idea what I was just saying, or why.

"Miss Wainwright?" the judge prompts, arching one eyebrow. Panic is seizing my stomach. This reminds me of my very first court appearance, many years ago now, when my knees had trembled so violently that I thought I would collapse behind the podium. Worse, I had twice trailed off while fumbling through my index cards, trying to decipher my own cryptic notes. But this is entirely different. I feel like one of those eraser boards I played with as a child. Yank up the plastic sheet, and all the words disappear. The contents of my mind seem irretrievably lost.

"I'm sorry, your Honor . . ." I say, relieved that my powers of speech have returned. But then, the apology is well-rehearsed. I'd say I've perfected it at this point. Just last week another judge, apropos of nothing, challenged me (in a smug, accusatory tone) to name the defensive line of the Green Bay Packers. Bewildered, I confessed my ignorance while opposing counsel chortled behind one hairy-knuckled hand. The judge shook his head in a disgusted way, as if this exchange had something to do with the merits of my client's position. What could I do but apologize? Sometimes an apology is your only recourse when you're grappling with the absurd.

The judge is at a loss. "Are you unwell?" he asks suspiciously. I'm not sure, so I nod my head. Realizing that "I'm sorry" is the full extent of my current vocabulary, the judge mercifully re-schedules the hearing and tells me he hopes I feel better soon. Henry's face is mottled as he tugs at my arm and whispers: "What the hell's the matter with you?"

Fair question.

I fly back to Milwaukee that evening, using my time in the air to convince myself that I don't need to see a doctor, after all. I can be very persuasive, even for a trial lawyer. Although my lapse was unprecedented, I concoct a laundry list of benign explanations. Five hours of sleep, no breakfast or lunch, and an overdose of caffeine laced with nicotine might account for such a reaction. I ignore the fact that this describes nearly every day of my adult life, and promise myself to start taking vitamins. Get back to the gym. Floss more often. Things like that.

I deplane reassured of my sanity, and roll my suitcase out to the parking structure. Miraculously, I remember the section where I parked my car without even checking my ticket. Further proof that my mind has returned, shame-faced, from its tiny detour down dementia alley. Except for one thing. When I get to that section, my car's not there.

I check my ticket. This is the right spot – 4G North. For several moments I just stand there, hoping my car will magically appear. (This happens sometimes when I'm ransacking the apartment for my Dictaphone or my eyeglasses; they suddenly materialize in a place I've checked at least twice before. So I'm hopeful.)

Eventually I find myself in a small, windowless room under fluorescent lights, describing my predicament to the airport security guy. He cocks his head and narrows his eyes before he interrupts me.

"A gray Jag?" he asks.

I stop mid-complaint and nod. The suggestion of a smirk compresses his lips, but concern creases his brow, too.

"A guard found the car in 4G North. Wednesday night, a little after eight. The engine was running, keys in the ignition. Lights were on. And the driver's side door was wide open." He's staring at my dumbstruck face. "We were worried about a car-jacking gone sour, something of that nature."

I rifle through my purse and sure enough, my keys are missing. *So this is what it's like to lose your mind,* I think to myself. Despite my sudden antipathy for the airport security guy, I don't want him to think me crazy. This is vitally important for some reason. So I clench my teeth and fake a smile.

"I'm so sorry," I say. "I was late for my flight."

***

I refuse to telephone Jason. This decision leaves me in the unenviable position of having no one to call.

Jason is my only real friend at the firm, and consequently, my only real friend. You don't bill 2800 hours a year and maintain many relationships outside the office. That kind of dedication has made me only the second woman partner at *Riley, Rudapeck*. The first was a lesbian they hide away in the obscure Baltimore office, where she services one very loyal client, and poses no threat of subjecting the firm to the inconvenience or expense of a maternity leave. In contrast, my soft-featured, serious face is conspicuous in every firm marketing photo. There should be a yellow sticker on my forehead marked Exhibit A: the only tangible evidence of equal opportunity for women at the firm. My position as token female partner did not come quickly or easily. For years I languished as a top-performing associate deemed "not quite ready" for partnership. My elevation to partner came two months after I let it slip that my tubes were tied. I am not charitable or naïve enough to believe that this was a coincidence.

Severing my fallopian tubes had another, paradoxical, effect. It led me to end my romantic entanglement with Jason, not just temporarily, but for good this time.

My relationship with Jason has always been off-kilter. We've fallen in and out of love, in a syncopated way, for years. Like children on a wooden teeter-totter, we're engrossed in a game that works only if one of us is down when the other is up. Lately, though, I've tried to slip off the contraption, and nurse my splinters, without letting Jason crash to the ground. My better angels want Jason to find a woman who's right for him, one with a maternal instinct and all her reproductive organs intact. Meanwhile, my selfish demons are prodding me to pick up the phone.

It's a dilemma for someone with only one friend. So naturally, I relent.

"Hey, you," I say when Jason answers.

"When did you get back?" The pleasure in his voice at hearing from me never fails to give me a twinge. The feeling is one part guilt, two parts yearning – a bittersweet, nostalgic sensation that is not entirely unpleasant.

"Just walked in." I take a deep breath. "Funny thing happened on my way to a dismissal." I describe my cryogenic performance at the hearing, working for a laugh, but Jason is not amused. The parking fiasco provides better material, until I notice my voice cracking.

"You've got to see a doctor," he says. He's adopted a paternal tone that the orphan in me craves at this moment. I try to think back, but after twenty-five years, the timbre of my father's voice eludes me. A few years ago, in a futile attempt to jog my memory, I actually visited my parents at their twin gravesites. Crouching in the brown, brittle grass, I hugged my coat against the wind and contemplated the identical dates of death etched on each grave marker. The cemetery was deserted, though, even by memories. A testament to our aloneness, I thought. I feel lucky, in a way, to have learned the truth at such a young age. I know people who are still shocked by abandonment, who still deny its inevitability. Hearts just waiting to be broken.

"Claire? Did you hear me?" It's reassuring to know that Jason can sense my nod. In the moment of silence that follows, we have an unspoken conversation. I know he wants to offer to come with me to the doctor. He knows I will balk at this. He will insist and I will firmly decline his offer. We do not need to actually have this conversation, both knowing exactly how it will go. So we don't speak. We just hang on to our receivers and listen to each other breathe. I suspect that this is the real reason spouses find less and less to say to each other as the years go by. When you really know someone, communication becomes telepathic.

The next morning, I have my secretary make an appointment with the gate-keeping physician that I picked at random from an HMO booklet last summer. At the time, my selection criteria were few and pragmatic: I wanted a female gynecologist with an office near mine. Leslie Tate, M.D. practiced three blocks away. That's all I knew about her. At the time, it was enough.

Apparently Dr. Tate has plenty of openings, which should give me pause, but I want this over with. So the next day during my lunch hour, I hurry three blocks down the wind tunnel of Wells Street in my pumps, clutching a briefcase, to my mystery doctor's office. It's my first visit, so in the hushed waiting room, I fill out a long questionnaire on my medical history by running a vertical line through all the "No" boxes, except two: Have you ever lost consciousness? Have you ever been pregnant? Those I leave blank.

In deference to waiting room etiquette, I've taken a seat in the corner so as to leave an empty space between my nearest neighbor and me. My vinyl chair is wedged against a large, fern-like plant that drapes over my arm as I write. The tiny leaves jiggle, shed a little dust on my sleeve, like dandruff. But the plant bothers me for some other reason I can't quite pinpoint. So I grasp a leaf with my fingertips, use my thumb to wipe the surface. Plastic. I tell myself that it doesn't mean a thing. But it's disquieting to realize your doctor can't be entrusted with real plants.

The *snap-snap* of my briefcase clasps springing open is familiar but loud, like shots fired in the subdued room, and cause an elderly man to flinch. I pull out a deposition transcript to stare at while I wait. Concentration is difficult despite the quiet. I have read the same incomprehensible sentence six times when the nurse calls my name, and leads me through the labyrinth of hallways to an examining room.

"Strip," she says like a kindly drill sergeant, "and put this on." She pulls the door closed on her way out. Obediently, I shed my clothes and don the paper gown.

Perched on the stiff paper ribbon that rolls over the examining table, I am impatient for the doctor to arrive and confirm my latest diagnosis. (At this point I'm thinking inner ear infection.) Cold air seeps through the gap in my gown along my spine. Flanking my knees, two clunky metal stirrups glint like the progeny of medieval torture devices. Bouncing one bare heel against the base of the table, I scan the posters that decorate the walls around me. In one, a teenaged couple lean together by a ubiquitous brick wall (read high school), blissfully unaware of the STDs they will soon transmit by way of unsafe sex. On the opposite wall, a young woman with old eyes and a distended belly stares from her poster to warn against the perils of the unwanted pregnancy. *Too little, too late*, I think to myself. *By the time you sit here, these posters can only mock you.*

Two short raps and the door swings open with a whoosh. It takes me a second to realize that Dr. Leslie Tate is a man. At least, I assume he's a man. He looks about twelve years old to me. It's a sure sign of age, this reaction on my part. But when you don't have children of your own, you don't realize when you've slipped into the next generation.

Dr. Tate asks his questions, pokes and prods, just like a real doctor. I politely decline the gynecological exam, indicating that the problem is somewhere north of his terrain. Finally, in exasperation, I tell him that I just need a referral my HMO might deign to recognize when the bills come.

I leave Dr. Tate's office with two things: a referral to a neurologist, and a name for my recent lapses. Seizure, he speculates, a word I fixate on for the next several days, until a blurry succession of neurologists and oncologists and surgeons give me a much scarier word on which to obsess.

They want to admit me to the hospital immediately, but I insist on going home to retrieve my briefcase and my toothbrush. Then, reluctant to leave my apartment, I procrastinate by – of all things – watering my plants.

***

The hospital admissions clerk seems distressed that I am checking myself in, alone, and asks me repeatedly if there is anyone she can call. I shake my head and retreat to the chairs, where I find another medical history form in the sheaf of admission papers. This time I check each box individually, and answer as if I am under oath. Even so, I leave two boxes blank. Being a lawyer, I'm well aware that not every question can be answered with a simple "yes" or "no."

***

On my back, I watch the succession of tubular lights and speckled ceiling tiles stream overhead as my gurney rolls toward the operating theater. An unfamiliar draft cools the shaved area at the top of my head. My surgeon is walking and talking beside me as we move down the corridor, but his words are indecipherable, spoken in the language of people who know, with reasonable certainty, that they will live to see another day. A language I seem to have forgotten, like my high school German.

It's good to be out of my hospital room. Away from the cloying smell of gladiolas delivered early this morning in a foil-wrapped vase. A bouquet from the firm, with a typed message on the card: *Get Well Soon. Riley, Rudapeck & Crane, S.C.* The phone by my bed rings now and then, but I don't answer it. Since check-in I've made only one call, to my Department Head, Kingston Bell.

Kingston was my mentor, once. That is, until his wife was overcome by her suspicions. She actually cold-called my number while checking random entries on her husband's cell phone bill. It's not me, I wanted to scream at her; it's the chain-smoking paralegal in Estate Planning! Did she really think I found her paunchy husband irresistible? There's nothing untoward in my relationship with Kingston, unless you count a minor episode of elevator-groping years ago in a Memphis hotel, somewhere between the 2nd and 14th floors, after a largely liquid dinner. But his wife is a nervous member of that shrinking minority, first wives of firm partners. So when I call Kingston this time, I don't tell him much, just the name of the hospital and the estimated length of my stay. His initial irritation at hearing from me softens a bit, and we work out the details on who will cover my cases while I'm (as Kingston puts it) "indisposed."

The nurse has given me something to calm my nerves, but my thoughts are still straying into dark corners. *What if I'm already dead? What if they're wheeling me to the morgue?* It hits me, then, why I've always wavered between burial and cremation. My dilemma stems from the cynical suspicion that an iota of consciousness survives, just a remnant of awareness, even after we're officially declared dead. And so the choice becomes, would I rather be burned alive or buried alive? I feel, suddenly, as if I've made a profound discovery – no less than the origin of Man's conception of Hell. And I think, *where's my Dictaphone? I should get this down.* I'm still groping in my gown for the little black recorder when they finally put me under.

Personally, I don't believe in Heaven or Hell, except for the ones we create for ourselves, right here on Earth.

***

After the surgeon leaves my room, I push myself up on the pillows, find my purse in the nightstand, and fish out a mirror. Holding it at arm's length, I survey the bandage wreathed around my stapled head; the impression is faintly Islamic. I wonder idly if I'll find religion, now that my life is engulfed by uncertainty. Shouldn't an atheist hedge her bets at a time like this? *Now wait just a minute,* I scold myself, *thirty-six-year-old women don't die of brain cancer.* I think this despite the surgeon's low-throated verdict: malignant, not benign; treatable, not curable. There was more, but it escapes me now. I just remember watching his lips move, hiding and exposing his coffee-stained teeth.

"Claire," Jason says from the doorway. Lanky and round-shouldered, he only looks like a sapling. On the inside he's a redwood, ancient and rooted.

"Hey, you," I say, and smile when Jason pulls a handful of spring flowers out from behind his back like an apprentice magician. The stems are wrapped in a soggy paper towel inside a rubber-banded plastic bag. Jason gardens. Despite my dismal track record – we both refer to my apartment as "the place where plants go to die" – he regularly replaces my withered, yellowing plants with tender green ones. But this offering is something else again. He hasn't presented me with flowers like this for six years, since the night he proposed, and I balked, while the lilies seemed to wilt in his fist. We differed, then, on the true course of love, and the proper response to an unplanned pregnancy. It took Jason six tumultuous weeks to win over my mind and heart, only to have my body decide the thing, and in the process, bloody more than the upholstery on my vintage sofa. Looking back, those six weeks were the worst of my life. And yet I had never felt more exhilarated or hopeful. I was certain, when they ended, that I would never feel that way again.

Jason finds a water glass to hold the blooms: daisies, daffodils, petunias, tulips. No lilies, though, not a one.

"So what's going on here?" Jason asks as he scrapes a chair up to my bedside. "Kingston seems woefully uninformed." He squints at my head bandage, and takes my hand.

"Brain tumor." It's the first time I've said this out loud, so I form the words experimentally, like I'm practicing my German for a trip abroad.

Jason blinks rapidly and his hand goes limp. Then he recovers himself and gives my fingers a bone-crushing squeeze.

"So, they operated, right? Removed it?" he asks.

"Part of it. The part they could reach. Seems it's grown roots, stubborn ones, like a dandelion."

"Oh, Claire." He looks so devastated that I rally a bit.

"I don't want to dwell on it now." I extract my hand from his to push myself up again in my bed. He half-stands, looking anxious, wanting to help, but I wave him back down. "Tell me what's happening," I say, almost chipper. "I'm in withdrawal here."

"You don't want – "

"I do, Jason. Except for these staples," I say, touching my bandage, "I feel fine. Really." He settles uncertainly in his chair.

"But – "

"C'mon, it's been more than a week. I'm starved for news. Give me something."

Jason shifts in his chair, crosses his legs at the knee. "Well, let's see. We did the postmortem on the Riley case this morning." He colors a little, uncrosses his legs, gamely stumbles on. "Cayhill got crucified."

Now this is more like it. We've re-focused on somebody else's misery.

"Who drove in the nails?" I ask.

"Bell and Minahan, mostly." He's being vague, uncomfortable with this line of questioning.

"And the sins?" I prompt.

"The usual. Missed opportunities. Wrong focus at a critical stage."

Those airy phrases slap me like hurricane-force winds. And I am completely unprepared.

My eyes well up and Jason blurs.

"Claire? What is it?" His hand covers mine while I try to swallow. Jason has only seen me cry once, last year while we were shopping. That time, I was undone by a pyramid shoe display. Drawn by the women's running shoes around the base, it took a moment for my eyes to move up to the apex, as the shoes shrank to smaller and smaller sizes. At the top of the display, a tiny pair of baby sneakers dangled from their shoelaces. The shrinking shoes on this tapering display gave the illusion of perspective, like a road narrowing into the distance. A road I had traveled already, running headlong and blind in the wrong direction. Undone by baby shoes, I had wept soundlessly while Jason's arms wrapped around me from behind.

It's funny. Back in that shoe store, Jason seemed to understand the reason for my tears before I did. And now, as he squeezes my hand, I recall the rest of my talk with the surgeon, the unbearable part that had eluded me before.

I close my eyes and ask him the Question. Hidden in the shadows, a phantom chorus of my un-wed husband, my un-conceived children, and my un-found friends hold their collective breath. We aren't fooled by his mealy-mouthed evasions. We can see the Answer in his eyes, and it is measured in months, not years.

Jason watches my tears drop, his face a mask of horrified comprehension.

"I'm sorry," I say. For once, it does not sound rehearsed.

64 Crayons

Dear Daddy, when are you coming home? Mommy won't get out of bed.
Love, Stevie

Dear Stevie, it might be a while before we can see each other again. But I'm always thinking about you. Be nice to mommy until she feels better. I love you, son. Dad

Dear Daddy, I sent you a pitcher of Mommy in her yellow bathrobe and red eyes. I drew it myself with my new crayons. The box has 64 colors but I only used three so far. Did you get it?

Dear Son, your picture is taped to my wall. It's a fine picture. Don't be afraid to use all the colors in your crayon box.

Dear Daddy, Mommy says you won't come home for a long, long, long, long time. Mommy has a job now with a pink dress and a name tag that says Mary but her name is Krystal not Mary. Why does her name tag say Mary? She says sometimes you don't want people to know your reel name. If you come home, maybe she can be Krystal again. Why won't you come home?

Dear Stevie, I can't leave this place right now. I would come home today if I could. Don't worry about the nametag. She's Mommy no matter what her nametag says.

Dear Daddy, Mommy sold our house so now we live in a partmint. I have a bedroom but Mommy sleeps on a couch in the front room. A mattress goes in and out of the couch like the shovel on my dump truck. We eat in the kitchen because we don't have a dining room anymore and Mommy sold the table and chairs and everything, even the piano, to Mrs. Timms, do you member her? So I don't have to take lessons with pukey Mr. Palmer anymore or practice my scales or anything. Yay! Can you come for a visit and see our new partmint? I can make scrambled eggs now by myself. If you come home I'll make scrambled eggs for you.

Dear Son, I remember Mrs. Timms from Church. She taught you Sunday school. Do you remember Mr. Krutz? The lawyer who came by the house a few times? He visited yesterday to tell me that I can't go home anytime soon. Believe me, son, I would if I could. I miss you and your mother terribly. Tell Mommy that I love her, would you, son?

Dear Daddy, I told Mommy what you said but then she cried, so I'm not going to tell her that anymore, okay? Also I don't like that Mr. Krutz. He picked me up once and his coat smelled like our carpet did after your party on New Years Eve member? Next time he comes over, don't let him come inside. If you look through the curtains first you can see it's him before you open the door. Mommy did that when the TV people came to our old house in vans with big white umbrellas on top. After that they didn't come anymore.

Dear Daddy, why don't you write to me? Mommy says she is getting a divorce. But you are still coming home, right?

Dear Daddy, did you get my letter? Are you mad at me? Mommy says no but her face was scrunched up.

Dear Daddy, Mommy has two jobs now. She answers the phone for a dentist office plus she is still a waitress at Hooligans. When she comes home she watches TV in the dark. I eat my dinner at Mrs. Timms' house when Mommy is at work. Last night Mrs. Timms made squash. It was orange and stringy and it tasted yucky. Bobby Timms said it looked like the guy who ate it before didn't like it either but then Mrs. Timms got mad and sent Bobby to his room. The kids at my new school are mean. Teddy Rugman says you're a jailbird. What does that mean? He took my napsack and dumped it out and all my stuff blew away in the wind. Write me back right away.

Dear Son, there are mean people everywhere. Watch your back, and don't take any guff from a snot like Teddy. The next time he touches you, sock him in the nose.

Daddy, what's a jailbird? I did what you said but the principal sent me home from school with a note and I can't go back for three days. Mommy is reel mad.

Daddy, are you still there? I heard Mommy tell Grandma that you are bitter cause you were tacked in the showers and had to go to the furmery for a month. We have tacks at school and they are sharp and pointy. Can I visit you at the furmery? What's bitter mean?

Dear Son, it means that you shouldn't listen to me about Teddy or anything else for that matter. I'm out of the infirmary now and I have a room all to myself, one without any tacks. But son, I don't think I can write to you for a while. I love you very much, and your mother, too.

Dear Daddy, next week is Career Week at my school. Tony's dad is coming to talk to us about being a shef which means a cook for rich people. And Rupert's mom who's a nurse, and Teddy's dad who's a lawyer, and Rachael's dad who is something but I forget. Can you come and talk to my class? Mommy says you were an animal nactifist before you went away. Also, you sold urbs at your store. When I grow up, I want to be a nactifist too. What's a nactifist?

Dear Daddy, did the tacks hurt your fingers? Write back. Love, Stevie

Dear Daddy, did you get my letter? Today our class went to the zoo on a feel trip. We saw giraffes and polar bears and dolfins and we ate cotton candy and rode on the train. Teddy Rugman says you are behind bars just like the gorillas. I was going to sock him but then I didn't. Do you have a tire swing? Can you come home now?

Dear Daddy, Mommy says your urb store belongs to Mrs. Feebler now because she gave us money for our half. Mommy says there are too many memrys in the store. I asked her and she says that memrys are everything you want to member and everything she wants to forget. She says we are making new memrys now. Are you making new memrys too? What do they look like?
Love, Stevie
P.S. I still don't know what memrys are but Mommy doesn't want to talk about it anymore.
P.P.S. Mrs. Feebler gave me a Monopoly game for my birthday. But she didn't smile or say happy birthday and she wouldn't eat any cake.

Dear Stevie, do me a favor. Find the Get Out Of Jail Free card in your Monopoly box. Next time you see Mrs. Feebler, give it her. Tell her it's a present from me to her husband Morris.

Dear Daddy, I did what you said but Mrs. Feebler got all red and yelled at Mommy that you made your own bed. Why is she mad if you made your bed? Mommy says your letters are a bad influants on me. Now she throws them down the garbage shute before she even opens them up. But I can still send letters to you. Mommy says she will mail them. Okay?

***

Dear Dad, I got an A on my History test today. I'm sending it so you can see the A. Sorry I don't write more but it's weird when you don't write back.

Dear Dad, it's Christmas Day and I had to string the lights on the tree and I couldn't figure out how. When I got done and plugged it in, all the lights stayed dark. I wish you could write and tell me how to string the lights.

Dear Dad, today was my first day at my new school, Truman Junior High. I was thinking about maybe trying out for the basketball team. But I'm probably not tall enough, and my free throws suck. So maybe not. Steve P.S. I'm bugging Mom to change her mind about the letters.

Dear Dad, Mom told me that you are in prison. I don't believe her. Please write back. Mom swears that she'll give me your letter this time, if you do. She says she won't even read it first. Your son, Steve

P.S. We moved back to Wisconsin last fall. The address is on the envelope just in case.

Dear Steve, your mother was right to chuck my old letters. You were too young and I didn't know how to explain things to you back then. Plus, my nerves were shot; I had some trouble adjusting to my situation here. And I guess I was angry about the divorce. But I don't blame her for that anymore. Your mother deserved a new life. What she says is true, son. I am in prison. My lawyer is working to straighten things out. Someday I'll explain. Now that your mother has lifted the letter ban, please write and tell me everything. We have a lot of catching up to do, and I worry about you. Love, Dad

Dad, you have a lot of nerve writing me that letter. After you lied to me all this time. I can't believe Teddy Rugman knew this stuff and you never even told me. Boy was I dumb. You don't have to worry about me anymore. I have a stepfather now, or didn't you know that? His name is Mark Mason and he's a great guy, unlike some people. He goes to all my basketball games and as soon as I get my learner's permit he's going to teach me to drive. He even bought me a rifle for Christmas and took me deer hunting with his buddies from the gun club. I'm just telling you this so you'll know why I don't want to write to you anymore. Steve
P.S. Mom told me what you did.

Steve, I don't know what your mother told you, but I didn't do what the jury said. It's true that I destroyed that lab; they were torturing defenseless animals there, all in pursuit of a better hairspray, a drier deodorant. My conscience compelled me to do that much. I suppose I was a fanatic in those days. But I didn't mean to hurt anyone. Morris and I thought the building was empty that night. You have to believe me, son.

Dad, I don't have to believe anything you say. Don't write to me anymore. If you're so innocent, how did you end up with a life sentence? Mom says you may never get out.

Steve, I had a lousy lawyer. The funny thing is, I knew he was lousy at the time. Yet I didn't fire him; I'm not sure why. I guess I thought my innocence would set me free. But my trial only lasted two days, and Krutz fell asleep twice, right in front of the jury. I can still see them smirking behind their hands. He didn't call any witnesses on my behalf. Not one. The kicker though was Morris, turning on me to save his own skin. He was so scared of going to prison that he flat-out lied. Took the stand and said that I knew the guard was there in the building that night. A good lawyer could have shaken Morris on cross, but I had to elbow Krutz just to wake him up. He didn't even get Morris to admit his sweetheart deal with the prosecutor – a lousy six years for the arson. Thanks to Morris, I went down on a murder rap. Together with the arson, that pretty much guaranteed me a life sentence. My new lawyer has appealed my case twice already. He says I have a good appeal but so far the courts don't agree. That's how I ended up in prison, son. I came here by railroad.

Dad, Mom says you're just making excuses. She also told me that your lawyer had a really loud snore. And that Morris Feebler is a sonofabitch, and you know Mom, she never swears. So I don't know what to think. But Mom says we've moved on and maybe you shouldn't write to me anymore. Steve

Dear Steve, I know I can't be much of a father to you from a prison cell, but let me try to do what I can. I've missed you very, very much these past seven years.

Dad, you don't even know me anymore.

Son, that's true I suppose. But I knew you once. I held you when you were ten minutes old and wrinkled as a prune. Pushed you in the park swings, high the way you liked it. Walked you to kindergarten, and taught you to ride your first bike, the red Schwinn with the training wheels. You were talkative and funny in a screwball way, and you held onto my thumb every time we crossed the street. People don't change all that much, son, when it comes right down to it. So I know a lot about you.

Ancient history, Dad. And if people don't change all that much, what does that say about you? Don't bother writing anymore. I mean it.

***

Dear Steve, I've left you alone for a long time now, but I hope you read this and think about it. I've done a lot of soul-searching lately, and I realize now that I never told you how sorry I am, for everything. For all the pain I've caused you and your mother. For messing up our lives so I couldn't be there for you when you needed me most. I'm grateful you have a stepfather like Mark to do for you what I cannot. It breaks my heart, and eases it, too.

Dad, I guess you didn't hear that Mark died. Three months ago while he was hunting. Heart attack. Mom won't get out of bed. So we've come full circle, you see? I'm graduating high school this spring and I can't wait to blow out of here. Milwaukee is such a bore. I hate shoveling snow. My girlfriend and I are going to California where it's sunny and the pot is cheap. Adios.

Dear Steve, I'm sorry about Mark. Try to be strong, for your mother's sake and for your own. If there's one thing I've learned in this place, it's that nothing deadens the soul like despair. So hold on to hope, son. Look at that old crayon box of yours. 64 colors, and only one of them black. Love, Dad
P.S. Have you thought about college?

Dad, that's a hoot, coming from you, the high school dropout.

Steve, I'll make you a deal. I'll get my GED in here if you try a year in college. What do you say?

Dad, aren't you too old for high school?

Steve, aren't you too young to give up?

I am not giving up!

Sure you are, son. What's wrong, are you afraid to break a sweat? I enrolled in the GED course here through the prison library. Why not send out a couple college applications and see what happens?

Dear Dad, I sent that application to UW-Madison, purely as a joke of course, but the funny thing is, they accepted me. My grades are only a B average but my test scores came out real high. And they liked the Student Court that I started at my high school. I told Daisy I can't go to California, and now she won't talk to me. Last night I saw her after the game talking to Roger Strobl, touching his arm and flipping her hair like she does when she's flirting. I went home and drank half a bottle of Jack Daniels and threw up all over the toilet. Then I slept on the cold tiles because they felt good and I couldn't get up. Today my head is pounding and my tongue feels like I licked out a sandbox.
P.S. I'm not sure anymore if college is for me.

Dear Steve, I know how hard it is to lose your first love.

Dad, who said anything about love?

Steve, you probably didn't know this, but your mother once dumped me for a medical student named Robert Morstad. Way back when she was in college and I worked at the health food co-op near campus. This was before we were married, of course. For a while there, I thought I would die. We had argued over my protest activities (she thought my *Make Love Not War* sign was silly) but the truth is she wanted a man with a future. So she went for a while with Morstad, a stiff who wore sweater vests and sent roses on Valentines Day. But it didn't last. Your mom and I were meant to be, despite our many differences. So don't give up on Daisy. True love is a force of nature, like rolling lava or a glacier's spread. Given enough time, it overwhelms all obstacles in its path.

Dad, I just got my first semester grades – a lousy 2.75 average. I'm practically on probation. Mom says I can't work all night and go to school all day and expect to do well when I'm falling asleep in class. I might as well drop out. Steve
P.S. Mom told me you're getting treatment for something in prison. Why didn't you tell me? Are you going to be okay?

Dear Steve, Don't worry about me, I'm feeling fine. But I've been wracking my brain in here, trying to think of some way you can pay for school. And then yesterday, in the yard, someone mentioned Joe DiMaggio. And I remembered the baseball cards my father gave me when I was a boy. God, I haven't thought of those cards in years. But my cellmate Curtis informs me that they're a hot commodity and might be worth something. So look in that old chest of mine, if you still have it. The cards should be in there. Maybe you can sell them.

Dear Dad, I found the cards. Man oh man – rookie cards in mint condition – the dealer I showed them to was drooling all over himself. But I feel funny about selling them, seeing as they were a gift from your Dad.

Dear Steve, Sell the cards. The greatest gift my father ever gave me was this chance to help my own son. I wish you could have known your grandfather. I used to think he was a hypocrite – a scientist with dreams of curing cancer who wound up working for a tobacco company – but he had his priorities straight. He didn't sacrifice his family to indulge some self-righteous whim. He was the kind of father I should have been. He put his family first.

Dear Dad, you've done okay, considering. And what's a man without his principles?

A free man, I expect.

Dad, I know you screwed up, but Mom says to err is human. I think she's forgiven you.

Son, does that mean you've forgiven me, too?

Dad, just so you know: I tried to track down Lyle Pinkett's family to give them the money from your cards. But all I could find was this second cousin in Cleveland who didn't even know Mr. Pinkett was dead. So I'm using the money for school, after all. It makes me sad, though. No one should die like that, all alone. Steve

Dear Son, I'm proud of you for trying to right my wrongs. Just remember: they're my wrongs, not yours.

Dear Dad, the University forces us to declare a major by our junior year, so I finally picked one: Criminal Justice. Ironic, no? Congratulations on your GED. Sorry about the appeal. What will your attorney try next? Steven
P.S. How are you feeling?

Dear Steven, I have a new lawyer, an expert on the Constitution named Arnold Toovey, who tells me that something called *ineffective assistance of counsel* is a very hot topic in the legal world these days. So he's petitioning the U.S. Supreme Court, and he says there's a chance the Court will agree to hear my case. Toovey's investigator has uncovered more dope on my narcoleptic lawyer. It turns out Krutz had a well-known problem with the bottle. There's a ton of complaints filed against him with the disciplinary board for lawyers. A few years ago, he stole thousands of dollars from an estate he was handling, and his license to practice law was suspended. That's all good, Toovey tells me. It's strange, how ass-backwards everything has become – the worse Krutz was back then, the better it is for me now. So here I am, sitting in prison, rooting for my first lawyer's incompetence, hoping for more news of his failings and faults. It's kind of crazy how the system works, but Toovey tells me you get used to it.

Dear Dad, I've decided I want to go to law school next year. Mr. Toovey says I can work at his firm in Austin this summer as a courthouse messenger. He tries to hide it but he's very excited about arguing your case before the Supreme Court. He's going to send me a pass so I can sit in the gallery, and Mom has offered to pay my airfare to Washington, D.C.

Steven, how is your mother?

She's mellowed out a lot since she went through "the change," as she would say. But she's lonely, I think.

Dear Dad, Mr. Toovey says any day now. I'm getting worried. Ever since the oral argument, my scalp won't stop itching. I've tried every dandruff shampoo on the market.

Son, it's out of our hands. Rub your head in burdock root oil. And get some biotin into your diet – try soybeans, garlic and avocados. Alfalfa and fava beans wouldn't hurt either.

Dear Steven, by now you've heard the news. But don't despair son. Toovey is taking this to the Governor. He can still commute my sentence on medical grounds, given my latest prognosis.

Dear Dad, I'm coming to see you. Governor Bruckner is a fucking moron.

Dear Son, don't come. All these years, we've managed fine without meeting face-to-face. And as much as I want to see you, I don't want you to see me. Not like this. Remember me the way I used to be, only better.
Love, Dad

***

Dear Dad, I'm a lawyer now. I was sworn in yesterday at the State Capitol. Governor Bruckner was there, and Arnold Toovey. And Mom, of course. Next month I start my job in the Public Defender's office. You'll never guess who I ran into at the County Justice Complex when I went for my interview. Daisy, remember her? She's a social worker for the County now; she finds homes for hard-to-place children, like kids who were abused or born with HIV. Last night she cooked me dinner — soybean something-or-other, a salad full of bean sprouts — and it felt like old times between us. She is as beautiful as ever. I wish you could have met her; you'd have liked her, I'm sure. She loves every species of animal. Keeps two bulldogs, a cockatoo, and a prehistoric-looking lizard named Charlemagne. And she's helped me to understand, in a way, how you could break into that lab with a crowbar and carry all those animal cages outdoors to pry them open. If only you hadn't gone back inside to pour gasoline all over the floor and light it with a kitchen match.   If only Lyle Pinkett hadn't gotten drunk, or passed out in the back office, or you had seen him, and rescued him like you did the rabbits.   If only Morris Feebler hadn't lied to trade his freedom for your life. Maybe then, you could have come home, all those years ago, to eat my scrambled eggs.   But none of that matters anymore.   I'm sitting cross-legged in Daisy's garden, writing this note to leave by your grave marker, so that you'll know, despite everything, that I love you.   I'm sorry I didn't say it sooner.   It's taken me such a long time to get here.   But today, after so many overcast days, the sun has a deep blue sky to itself.   And all around me the flowers are opening, red bleeding hearts and orange gladiolas, pink star-clusters, yellow daffodils.   The dragonfly darting near my hand has violet wings.   And Dad, I'm guessing you've persuaded God, as you once did me, to use all 64 of His crayons.

Your son always,

Steven

HOW I QUIT SMOKING

FRIDAY NIGHT I COME IN late, an hour after curfew. Mom is there, arms crossed, in the hall just outside the vestibule – blocking my way. She's wearing her ratty old bathrobe and a pair of pink slippers she bought for me but that I refuse to wear. I wonder if she'll notice my tights are missing. As I try to squeeze past her, she sniffs and wrinkles her nose.

"You've been smoking again," she says plaintively. It's true, I have, but denial is automatic at seventeen.

"We were at Gilroy's, listening to the band. I can't help it's smoky there."

Mom's washed off her pencil, and without eyebrows, she looks defenseless. "I suppose all your friends think smoking is *cool*," she says.

I wince at her slang, so '70's, so Mom. Nobody under thirty says "cool" anymore, not even the retro freaks at school in their bellbottoms and tie-dyed tee shirts. Any other night I'd argue with her, but just now, I'm not in the mood.

"I'm going to bed," I reply instead, trying to escape. But Mom puts her hand on my arm.

"You know how Robbie feels about you. I don't want him following in your footsteps." Stung by this, I shrug off her hand.

"Robbie doesn't know I'm alive." Another lie. It's me who ignores him. Mom's forehead puckers between her eyes and she pulls her robe tighter. Her skin is so dry I can see the scales on the back of her hand below her red knuckles. I wish she'd use some hand cream. She could manage that much.

I leave her there, clutching her bathrobe, and take the stairs two at a time. Slam the door to my bedroom and toss my jacket aside. The threadbare denim misses the chair and falls in a puddle on the floor, where a crumpled pack of Camels spills from the pocket. I scoop up the pack, fish in the pocket for matches, crack the window, and light up. I consider stuffing a towel under the door. But then I don't bother; Mom won't come in. She hates a scene. That's why she's so disturbed by me. I'm a provoker of scenes.

Knuckles rap, insistent, on my door. I curse under my breath, flick the cigarette out the window, wave my hand in the air, call out, "I'm changing." Swirls of smoke slipstream past my flailing hand.

"Corrine?"

My hand stills. "What do you want?" I sigh as the door swings open and Robbie slips in. He is wearing pajamas my mother picked out, filled with tiny biplanes suspended every which way in a blue cotton sky. The material hangs from his slim frame with an apologetic air.

No self-respecting fourteen-year-old would wear such pajamas. Robbie does it to please Dad by humoring Mom. She loves those stupid pajamas.

Robbie fidgets, pulls at the hem of his pajama top to no apparent purpose, and bounces up and down on the balls of his feet. He is – always has been – hyperactive, although they have a new name for it now. My parents have defied the doctors, refused the Ritalin, and set for themselves the thankless task of treating Robbie's condition with patience and attention. Dad, especially, when he's around, between his far-flung business trips. Mom means well, I suppose, but she's hapless.

"Dad's coming back tomorrow," Robbie says. "He's gonna take me to a Bucks game." Since the diagnosis of my brother's problem, Dad has spent most of his free time with Robbie. He has tried to teach his son a measure of self-control. I am Mom's project. It's like they've divvied up their children. I'm not sure who among us drew the short straw.

"How special," I sneer. "I'm so pleased for you." Robbie looks away, twists the hem of his pajama top. He starts to kick the side of my bureau with his curled toes. The banging must hurt but he keeps at it.

I relent a little, cast about for a peace offering. "Want a cigarette?" I say, holding out my crumpled pack. I know that some of his friends are smoking now. I see them experimenting with shaky smoke rings as they sit on the steps of the church down the street from his school.

Robbie stops kicking and squints at me. "I'm going to bed."

"You don't have to smoke it now," I say. "You can save it for later." He watches me shake out a dented cigarette and hold it out to him. Robbie takes the butt from me and hides it in the breast pocket of his biplane pajamas. "Okay," he says, opens the door and makes his escape.

***

Every Saturday morning, we have assigned chores to do. Robbie is raking dead leaves from the garage. Inside the house, I can hear the rake tines scrape across cement. I am stretched on the couch in the den reading *People* magazine. Mom flutters around me with a dust rag and a bottle of lemon-scented furniture polish. She has reminded me twice now to do the breakfast dishes. Bowls sit in the sink growing crusty with dried cornflakes.

"What's keeping your father?" Mom mutters under her breath. I decide that I'll start the breakfast dishes as soon as I hear his car tires on the driveway. But now the only sound is the scraping of my goody-two-shoes brother finishing his chores. Mom looks at her watch and her forehead puckers.

An hour later the telephone rings. I am still on the couch, but sitting now, peeling old nail polish in tiny strips from my fingernails. Mom is upstairs. She must answer the phone; at least, it stops ringing. I think I hear a small cry but decide I have not. Robbie comes into the den and sits on the couch beside me. He has washed his hands but slivers of grime remain under his nails.

Robbie stares at the infomercial for acne cream on the TV, knowing better than to ask whether he can change the channel. Instead, he rocks to and fro, and taps one foot near the skirt of the couch.

Mom comes down the stairs and into the den. I don't look up but Robbie does; he stops rocking and his tapping foot freezes. Mom lowers herself into the space between us and puts her arms around our shoulders. I'm so shocked by this gesture that I don't react.

"There's been an accident," she says, haltingly, "on the expressway. Your father . . ." Her voice is hoarse. Robbie and I hunch under her arms. "God," she breathes, "I don't know how to say this." Mom squeezes us to her ribcage.

Robbie's eyes are wide; his body still.

Mom takes a long shuddering breath. She finds a way to tell us that our father is dead.

Robbie stays frozen for several minutes — under ordinary circumstances, a small miracle.

***

The day of the funeral is unseasonably warm. I've lost track of what day of the week it is. Mom tells us to take showers, so we do, and at last the grime under Robbie's nails disappears. We pull dark clothes from our closets. I don't need to think because my clothes are mostly black anyway.

At the funeral home, the air is suffocating, steeped in the cloying, musty scent of drying flowers, air freshener and the heavy perfume of old ladies. I stand apart from the crowd and watch my mother submit to hand clasps and hushed condolences from people I don't recognize. I think that if my own hand were clasped that way, it would crumble like so much cigarette ash. At the front of the room, the casket rests on a pedestal. What looks like a heavily powdered rubber replica of my father lies inside, eyes closed, hands overlapping, expression placid. I glance at it from the corner of my eye, but I stay away.

An hour later, Mom finds me in the bathroom. I'm sitting on the edge of the sink smoking my last butt. "Where's Robbie?" Mom asks. She frowns, in a distracted way, at the furl of smoke rising from my cupped palm. I shake my head and shrug my shoulders at the same time: *don't know, don't care.* But I stand, douse my cigarette under the faucet and toss it with excessive nonchalance into a garbage can. Then I follow my mom out of the bathroom.

Mom sends Uncle Earl outside to find Robbie. When my brother finally sidles through the chapel door, alone, his hands are dirty and bright red blood drips from one nostril. Mom's penciled brows draw together. "What happened?" she asks in a tremulous voice. Robbie swipes a hand across his lip, smearing the blood onto his cheek, and stares at his shoes, sullen and mute. With a sigh, Mom sends him back to the family sitting room, behind a dusty velvet curtain, to wait out the viewing period with Grandma and Grandpa. I follow and sit beside him on the sofa. When our grandparents leave to join the line of mourners passing the casket before it is closed, Robbie tells me the whole story.

First he confesses to having thrown away the cigarette I gave him, the one he tucked into the pocket of his dopey pajamas. As it turns out though, he had tried smoking, twice, with his friends during lunch period, in response to a dare. He says it almost made him puke, and he returned to class shaky, with clammy hands. But then, at the funeral, he is standing at a window and spies a gas station across the street. And he thinks, why not? It'll only take a minute. So he slips out and darts through the traffic to the station. He figures he looks older in his suit, and kids his age buy cigarettes all the time, anyway.

The gas station attendant doesn't see it that way. *You're not buying any butts here, kid,* he tells Robbie, *so take a hike.* Robbie is undeterred.

"I just stand there," Robbie tells me now, "refusing to budge, and then the greaseball's eyes get slitty and he says, *Where you coming from, anyway?* He's noticing the suit, I guess. So I point across the street and say, *Bartlett's. My dad died.* And the guy starts shifting from foot to foot, and after about a century he finally says, *Sorry kid, but it's the law. You ain't sixteen.*"

At this point in the story, Robbie's eyes glaze over. "So I slug the jerk," he says, still plainly in awe of his own hubris. "He's a foot taller than me, but I never think twice. Shit, I don't think at all. I just take a swing, clip him pretty good, too, right in the cheek." My brother shakes his head. "He staggers back a step or two, this look of total shock on his face." A smile twitches at the corners of Robbie's mouth. "Then he lights into me. It's all over in about three seconds. I mean, the guy is practically twice my size. Next thing I know, he's pulling me off the floor. All apologetic, which ticks me off. *You alright?* he asks me, like he's really worried. I kind of nod because I'm not sure. *Then get the hell out of here,* he says. *And stop pickin' fights you can't win.* Like he's teaching me something I don't know. The moron." Robbie is shaking like an adrenaline junkie.

"Go clean yourself up," I say. I watch him until he disappears into the restroom. Then I leave through the velvet curtains, skirt the edge of the viewing room to the door and slip outside. I run across the street and into the gas station, where the greasy-haired attendant sells me a pack of Camels. A bruise blooms on his right cheek under the acne scars. "How did that happen?" I ask, pointing.

He touches his cheek gingerly with three fingers, the nails ragged. "Crazy kid," he says, then drops his hand quickly and straightens his back. Even so he's not much taller than me. "Tried to buy a pack of butts. I had to throw him out."

"He must have put up a fight," I say, oh-so-innocent.

"Yeah, well," the attendant stutters, "he sucker-punched me. I tell him I can't sell him nothin and he screams, *Who do you think you are, anyway?* Then he jumps me. The kid was pissed as hell about something."

"Weird," I say.

"Yeah," the attendant agrees, his eyes wandering to the window that faces the street and Bartlett's. Then he looks back at me. His lips are dry and peeling. "He even pulled a knife on me. He was a big kid, for his age. We wrestled a while. I got it away from him, no problem. Then I kicked his you-know-what." He examines his nails, waiting. I'm struggling hard not to laugh in his face.

He abandons his nails and looks around the floor. "The dumb kid made a hell of a mess." All I see is a half-tipped display of chewing gum, the packs scattered across the tile. "Guess who gets to clean it up?" the attendant says, morose now.

"I feel for you," I say, "you've had a rough day." I take a piece of bubble gum off the display, untwist the wrapper and pop the pink cube in my mouth. Then I drop the wrapper. We watch it flutter to the floor where it settles next to a pack of Juicy Fruit.

The attendant looks up and frowns at me. "You're wearing black," he says in a monotone.

"I always do," I say. It's the truth but he doesn't believe me anymore. I smile brightly and wave with my cigarettes on the way out.

I am back in the funeral home before Mom suspects a thing.

***

Robbie and I are in the alley behind Bartlett's. We sit on the curb next to an overflowing dumpster haloed by swarming flies. The gutter at our feet is choked with matted leaves and litter.

I stamp the pack on my palm to tighten the tobacco, pull the tiny cellophane strip and peel away the foil on the side without the Surgeon General's warning, always mindful of the superstition, passed on by my friends, against removing the foil from the side with the warning. This ensures that I won't die of cancer.

I light a cigarette and pass it to Robbie, then use the same match flame to light my own. Robbie sways back and forth and scuffs his new shoe against the pavement. Amateur that he is, he holds the cigarette between his thumb and index finger, like a straw, and sucks on it, tentatively at first. Then he tries to choke off his cough, but it comes through his nose in a staccato of grunts, punctuated by tiny bursts of smoke. I inhale deeply and blow a few smoke rings to show him the fruits of my expertise. Robbie doesn't seem to notice, though.

We sit in silence for several minutes, smoking. A sports announcer's voice drifts across the alley from the screen window of a neighboring house. A basketball game. The Bucks are playing. This is the day Dad promised to take Robbie to the game.

And it occurs to me then, that my father is dead. If he were alive, everything would be different. For one thing, Robbie and I wouldn't be sitting together on this curb. Robbie's nose wouldn't be bleeding again. I wouldn't be chewing this stale gum. My signature black outfit would not be so perversely appropriate to the occasion.

With a sidelong glance, I look at Robbie closely, for the first time in years, and see the fine hair on his upper lip. His shoulders are rounded, his back bowed, and his nostrils are pinched as the smoke from his cigarette rises and floats past his face. He does not look like the boy in the biplane pajamas. I wonder how Mom can possibly cope with both of us, now, alone.

I lean over and snatch the cigarette from Robbie's hand. "This is a one-time deal," I say. The butt hits the cement in a spray of sparks and I grind it under my heel, leave a smear of dented filter, torn paper and tobacco shreds. Robbie stares at me with narrow eyes. So I drop my own cig and grind again. Then I twist around and pitch the pack toward the dumpster. It arcs through space, sun glinting off the cellophane. "Three points," I say when it lands. Angry flies scatter and regroup, droning loudly in protest.

"Sure you want to do that?" Robbie asks.

"Let's get back." I stand up and brush debris off the seat of my skirt. "Mom will go ballistic if she finds out we're gone."

"Since when do you care?" Robbie looks incredulous.

I can't even begin to answer this question. So all I say is, "C'mon." And he follows me back inside.

A little later, Mom and I watch the pallbearers slide my father's casket into the hearse. Robbie is missing again. As it turns out, he is back in the alley, dumpster-diving for my Camels. But he won't tell me that story until much, much later, when it has long since been dwarfed by everything else he has done.

TRIPLE SOLITAIRE

ME AND BARKER ARE FINGER-PAINTING. We have three colors of paint that Grandma Purdue sent us, blue and yellow and red. Sissy is cutting out clothes for her paper doll. She has long curly hair that's hanging in her face the way Mommy hates. But Mommy is upstairs in her bedroom with all the curtains closed and the door too. We can't go in when the door's closed. That's a rule. Mommy has a hurt head sometimes and she closes the door and we can't go inside. If we knock she won't answer.

Barker and me are twins. We are the same except he is a boy. He can make pee standing up. I tried to once but I missed and made a puddle and Mommy got mad and said sit on the pot. Barker and me do everything but pee the same. Today we have on blue overalls and a red shirt. Daddy put blue socks on Barker and white socks on me. We traded and now we each have one white sock and one blue sock and we look the same. I put my hand in red paint and press on my paper like we did in school.

"What's that?" Barker asks me.

"A turkey."

"It's gonna be *Christmas*," Barker says. "Make an angel."

I don't know how to make an angel. We didn't make angels in school. I make a blue turkey with my clean hand. The blue turkey and red turkey face each other and they look the same like me and Barker. Barker is making swirls but they all look like muddy water in the middle.

Daddy is in the garage. He is warming up the car. When Mommy gets up we are going to church.

Sometimes Daddy and me and Barker play triple solitaire. We each have our own deck of cards. My deck has red checks and Barker's has blue checks and Daddy's has pictures of ladies with power tools. Daddy used to sell power tools before he stopped working. "I was downsized," he tells people, but he doesn't look any littler. Now he works on *projects* in the garage. He has a lot of power tools. They make loud noises and leave piles of sawdust on the garage floor. He is making a rocking chair and a birdhouse and something else but I forget. By the workbench there's a mean old Indian chief made of wood. The chief is tall like Daddy but his back is straight. His paint flakes all over like sunburn at the beach. Daddy says the chief used to sell cigars. Maybe the chief was downsized too.

Mommy told Grandma that Daddy is *despondent*. I don't know what that means but I think it's bad. I asked my teacher Missus Finkelstein and she said we could look it up in the big dictionary. I tried to look by myself but I couldn't do it and Missus Finkelstein said she'd help me later but she never did.

When Daddy and me and Barker play triple solitaire I always lose. Daddy is fast and Barker is messy. I try to keep the cards in a straight line. Daddy smiles and rubs my head. "You're persnickety," he says. I don't know what that means but I think it's good. I don't mind losing to Barker and Daddy. But sometimes I wish I could win like Barker.

I slide off my chair and pull my picture off the table. A blue dribble runs off the corner of the page and plops on my white sock.

"Where're you going?" Sissy says.

"To show Daddy."

"He said not to leave the table."

Daddy said that but I forgot. "I want to show him my turkeys." I don't know but I'm pretty sure they are persnickety turkeys.

"Daddy said not to go in the garage," Sissy says. She points her scissors at me. She looks like Mommy does when Mommy doesn't have a headache.

My eyes start to sting. I want to see Daddy and sit with him in the warm car. I sniff and rub my eye with my fist but Sissy is cutting out a red dress for her doll so she doesn't see. I climb back up on my chair.

The floor above us creaks. We all stop moving for a minute and listen to Mommy walk along the hall upstairs. She gets to the top of the stairs and comes down. We watch her through the hole in the wall where the telephone is. Mommy comes down one step at a time and holds the banister tight. Sometimes Barker and me slide down the banister. Barker slides fast headfirst on his stomach and I slide slow on my bum, a little at a time, but otherwise we slide the same. Mommy forgot to tie her robe and the tie is dragging behind her. She still has all the pins in her hair and some of the pins stick out sideways.

Mommy comes into the kitchen. She doesn't smile but her mouth stretches and her eyes crinkle up. Her hair looks like the middle of Barker's painting. Grandma Purdue says Mommy was a great beauty before she married that good for nothing but Mommy tells her to hold her tongue *in front of the children*. I held my tongue once but it was boring and I couldn't talk and my fingers smelled like my belly button so I let it go. Barker is an outie and I am an inny but otherwise our bellybuttons look just like each other.

"Do you feel better Mommy?" Sissy asks.

Mommy nods and goes to the coffee pot. Daddy made coffee for her this morning like he always does. He grinds beans and it's loud like his power tools. Daddy never drinks coffee because it makes him anxious. I asked Missus Finkelstein to look up *anxious* with me in the big dictionary and it was bad so I'm glad that Daddy doesn't drink coffee. Sometimes Barker drinks from Mommy's coffee cup when she's not looking. Barker likes coffee but I don't. Other drinks we like the same.

Mommy leaves with her coffee to go back upstairs. She is at the bottom of the stairs when the phone rings. She stops and stands there with her eyes closed. Her eyelids are purple. I count the rings, one, two, three, four, but not out loud just in my mouth. Mommy's eyes open like butterflies and she comes back to the phone. We watch her through the hole in the wall.

"Hi, Mom," she says. Grandma Purdue lives in Seattle and calls us every Sunday. Now Mommy bends down to peek at us through the hole in the wall. Sissy picks up her scissors to cut out a coat she drew for her paper doll. Barker dips his fingers in red and swirls them in muddy circles. I hold up my turkeys to show Mommy but she doesn't look. She stands up again and all I can see is her coffee cup on the shelf by the phone and her hand twisting the curly cord around and around her wrist.

"Not really," Mommy says, "but I took something."

Mommy told me both my grandmas are widows. That means they don't have grandpas anymore but I don't know why. I never saw Grandpa Purdue except in pictures. There's one on Mommy's dresser where he is standing with his round hat in both hands. My other grandpa is Grandpa Moss. I remember him from when we visited his house one time. We were supposed to go for dinner but we left before we ate anything. Grandpa Moss is big with curly hairs in his nose and he had a funeral last year. Daddy went with Barker and Sissy but I had white spots on my tonsils and stayed home with Mommy. She let me eat ice cream whenever I wanted. I like butter pecan the best. Barker likes neapolitan but we both like ice cream better than anything.

"I'm not sure. In the garage, probably . . ." Mommy leans down again. "Kids, where's your Daddy?" The phone is pressed between her cheek and her shoulder.

"In the garage!" Barker and me say. We look at each other and giggle. We like it when we talk together. It used to happen all the time but now it hardly ever does.

We can hear the crackly sound of Grandma Purdue talking through the phone and the *hhehh* of Mommy sighing.

"He's fine, Mother, really. Have a little faith." Sissy stops cutting and looks up. "Well, he's bound to find something."

Barker is painting a new picture but it looks like his first picture because all the colors are mixed together and turning brown.

"I already told you, he won't go." I look through the hole in the wall and the curly cord winds all the way up to Mommy's elbow. Grandma Purdue always says that Daddy is tightly wound and I guess now Mommy is too. "He has the doctor's number. But really, Mother, it's up to him."

I scrunch down in my chair and look up at Mommy through the hole. She's pinching the top of her nose.

"I don't want to talk about that right now." Mommy takes her hand away and sees me. I smile at her. She turns around so all I see is the back of her grayish bathrobe. There's tiny strings pulled out of it all over. Mommy's voice goes soft and mumbly. "Because the kids are right here."

Mommy is unwinding the cord from her arm like Daddy unwinding the garden hose. "Because I haven't decided yet, that's why." Mommy turns around again like she wants to hang up. "Well, Mother, you never did. That's always been obvious." *hhehh*. "Look, I've got to go change. We're going to miss church." *hhehh*. "Me too." Mommy hangs up the phone and picks up her coffee cup. She goes down the hall and up the stairs, holding the banister.

Barker says Grandpa Purdue and Grandpa Moss are both dead but I don't believe him. Barker and me talk the same but sometimes Barker tells lies.

Barker told me lies after Grandpa Moss's funeral. He told me that Grandpa Moss laid on his back in a coffin and Barker touched his face and it was cold and powdery. I said we should ask Grandpa Moss why his face was cold but Barker said we wouldn't ever see Grandpa Moss again. I said Barker you're a big fat liar and Barker said you're a retard and that was the first fight we ever had ever. That night Barker wet his bed. In the morning Mommy washed his sheets. The next night he wet his bed again. Barker and me do everything the same. The third night I drank a big glass of water. I woke up in the middle of the night and I had to pee. I was sleepy so first I got out of bed. Then I remembered and crawled back under the covers. I tried to let go of my pee but it was harder than I thought. So I pretended I was sitting on the pot and then the warm wet spread under my bum and down my legs. First it felt good but then it felt like wearing my wet swimming suit on a cold day. I got up and went to Mommy and Daddy's room and shook Mommy and told her I wet my bed just like Barker.

Mommy put plastic on our mattresses. She plugged nightlights in the walls by our beds. My nightlight was Cinderella and Barker's nightlight was Spiderman but otherwise our nightlights were the same. We wet our beds every night for five nights. I counted. Barker and I wet our beds the same except he did it by accident and I did it on purpose. On the sixth night I wet my bed and Barker didn't. So then we both stopped wetting our bed.

We don't talk about Grandpa Moss anymore. I don't know where he is. We don't see Grandma Moss either because she's in a home for people in Wisconsin who don't remember things anymore. Daddy visits her there sometimes but we don't go along.

Sissy holds up her paper doll with a long black fuzzy-looking coat tabbed to the shoulders and waist. "It's a mink," Sissy says. "Her husband owns a lumber mill and has wads and oodles of money." Grandpa Moss has three lumber mills in Wisconsin where Daddy grew up. Daddy didn't want to work in a lumber mill and that's why the lawyers for Grandpa Moss didn't give Daddy any money after his funeral. Sissy heard Mommy telling Grandma Purdue on the phone.

Sissy visited Grandma Purdue in Seattle not last summer but the summer before that. I don't really remember but that's what Sissy told me. She got to fly in an airplane all by herself with a note safety-pinned to the collar of her dress. When Sissy got home she called Daddy a loser and Mommy slapped her and Sissy cried. Barker and me were supposed to visit Grandma Purdue last summer but then we didn't.

I am sick of making turkeys with my hands. I wonder what animal my foot will make. Maybe it will look like an angel. The paint pan spills a little when I slide it off the table and put it on the floor. With my thumb I peel off my white sock with the blue drips on it. The paint in the pan now is dark purple because I mixed the red with the blue. I put my bare foot in the pan and then on the paper. Between my toes it's purple like Mommy's eyelids. I press down hard and count to five.

When I lift my foot it's sticky at first but then the paper floats back to the floor. My footprint is pretty but it doesn't look like an angel.

The last time I made footprints was on the beach with Daddy. We went to the beach after Grandpa Moss's funeral when Mommy told Daddy you could have swallowed your pride but it's too late now. It was March and windy and cold. Mommy didn't want to go.

"We should conserve our resources," she said. That's how Mommy talks in front of the children.

"I need to get away," Daddy said. He was still tall but his shoulders sagged down and when they talked he never looked at Mommy's face.

hhehh. "Should we invite the Osgoods?" Missus Osgood is Mommy's best friend. Mister Osgood used to work with Daddy at the power tool company. We take all our vacations with the Osgoods.

Daddy shrugged. "I don't care." Daddy says that a lot, like when Mommy asks what do you want for dinner or the white shirt or the blue or should we cash the check from mom? He didn't used to say it so much but now he does.

The Osgoods didn't come. We stayed in a cabin with crackly paint and a saggy porch with wind chimes that tinkled all the time until Mommy cut them down with a scissors. She said they made her head hurt. It was cold outside so we played board games in front of the heater. Daddy tried to teach Sissy chess but she only liked the queen so they quit. Then Daddy stood up and stretched and said he was going for a walk on the beach and did anyone want to come? Nobody said anything.

The only sound was the wind outside and the click-click of the heater. It made me feel funny like when Mommy has a headache and I knock on the door and she doesn't answer. When Daddy opened the cabin door I ran after him and tugged on his coat sleeve.

"I want to go with you, Daddy."

"Alright, squirt. Grab your coat."

It was cold outside. The wind made Daddy's hair stand up. He took long steps and I ran to keep up. We went down to the water. Daddy sat down on the hard sand and untied his shoes. He pulled off his socks and stuffed them into his shoes and rolled up his pants until the dark hair showed on his legs. He stood up holding his shoes on two fingers. He took my hand.

"Stay above the water line, now," he said. "You don't want to catch your death." I walked near the seaweed the waves left behind. Daddy's bare feet made big prints in the damp sand. Little waves with white foam spilled over his toes sometimes and sometimes they didn't reach that far. My saddle shoes sank in the sand. I tried to walk in a straight line. The wind was cold but Daddy's hand was big and warm. I knew I wouldn't catch my death as long as Daddy held my hand.

"Daddy? Did Grandpa Moss catch his death?"

Daddy squinted even though there was no sun in our eyes. "He was just old, squirt. Like they talked about at the funeral."

"I had white spots. Mommy gave me butter pecan ice cream."

"That's right."

"Daddy? What happens when you die?"

Daddy's steps slowed down so I could keep up better. "No one really knows, squirt."

We walked for a long long time. My arm ached but I didn't let go of Daddy's hand. Daddy stared out at the line where the gray sea met the gray sky. Once he stopped to tie my shoe. My laces were sandy.

"Daddy, why wouldn't the lawyers for Grandpa Moss give you any money?"

Daddy waited before he answered. "My father and I didn't get along."

"Why not?"

"We were nothing alike."

We kept walking until we reached some rocks. The wind was cold and I was shivering. There were white signs with red letters standing everywhere in the rocks. All I could read was "NO." The rocks were dark gray with white streaks from the seagulls.

"What do they say?" I asked Daddy. He read the signs.

"Time to head back."

We turned around. Daddy looked down the beach. He let go of my hand and was quiet for a while.

I looked at the beach. One set of prints dotted the sand. They went back and forth by the wavy line of seaweed. But Daddy's footprints were all gone. Just smooth wet sand and pieces of shell here and there. A wave rushed in and slid up the sand. The foamy water came near my shoe prints but stopped and went back to the sea.

A funny feeling made my throat hurt. Like back in the cabin when nobody said they wanted to walk with

Daddy only a hundred times worse. My shoe prints looked all crooked and alone and I didn't want to be all alone without Daddy.

We looked at the beach and I sniffled.

"There's your answer, squirt," Daddy said at last. He waved his hand at the smooth sand where he had walked. "You die and it's like you were never here at all." His hand dropped to his side like it was too heavy.

I tugged on his sleeve. "Make more footprints, Daddy." My eyes got hot and blurry. Daddy just stared at the sea.

"It's peaceful here," he said, but not to me.

A wave crashed on the beach. The wind made my face sting. I started to cry. Daddy looked surprised. He picked me up and held me on his hip like he did when I was little. I tucked my head in his neck. He held my head between his cheek and his shoulder like Mommy holds the phone. I stopped crying and started to hiccup. Daddy patted my back. By the time we got back to the cabin my hiccups were gone.

I don't want to make footprints anymore. I want to show Daddy my persnickety turkeys. I wish the car would warm up. I stand on my chair to see out the kitchen window. I try to see Daddy in the garage. But the little windows in the garage door are cloudy like the mirror after Daddy takes his shower. It must be warm in the garage.

Mommy walks into the kitchen. I didn't even hear her coming. She goes to the coffee pot, still in her bathrobe but tied now, kind of. She pours a cup of coffee and looks at my purple toes on the seat of the chair.

"Don't go tracking that paint all over the house."

"I won't, Mommy."

"We're going to skip church," she says. "Stay home with Daddy." *hhehh*.

I watch the little puffs of steam come out of Mommy's coffee cup. I want to tell Mommy something but I don't know what. "Why does your coffee make clouds?" I say.

Mommy's eyes get crinkly. "Because it's warm."

I look at Mommy and she looks at me. I say, "Daddy's been warming up the car." Mommy looks frozen and her knuckles get white on the handle of her cup. I look out the window. Clouds are puffing from under the garage door. Mommy looks out the window too and makes a funny sound. She drops her coffee cup on the floor and it smashes and the spilled coffee looks like Barker's painting.

Through the window I see Mommy running down the driveway. Her bathrobe blows behind her like the flag on our flagpole. She runs to the garage and yanks open the side door with both hands and all the clouds float out. My legs feel wobbly so I bend my knees and sit down on the chair and hug my legs.

Sissy goes to the back door that Mommy left open. Cold air blows in around her. Sissy starts to cry loud like a baby. Everything gets loud and fast and Mommy calls on the phone and she's breathing funny and men come and carry away something under a blanket. I think maybe it's the Indian chief. Barker and me hold hands and follow Mommy around the house.

The men leave with the Indian chief but no siren like when they came. Mommy sits us at the dining room table and tells us something about Daddy but I don't know what. Mommy is crying and Sissy too. Barker and me go upstairs while Mommy calls Grandma Purdue.

"Where is Daddy?" I ask Barker.

"You're such a retard." Barker's face is splotchy red. He talks about Daddy but I cover up my ears.

Later I see my purple footprints all over the house. They look funny because my purple foot made footprints but my clean foot didn't. Barker asks me if I want to play double solitaire with him but I say you're too messy, Barker. When I see Daddy I will hold his hand and tell him that Barker and me are *nothing alike* either. I like butter pecan and sliding slow on the banister and making persnickety turkeys. Barker is a liar.

HERE I AM

THEY SENT ME TO THIS place after the trial. I like it here, in a way. When the human freak show starts to wear on my nerves, I just duck out the nearest exit. (They're supposed to be locked, but some orderlies prop the doors open with rocks so they can sneak outside for a smoke.) It's quiet on the grounds, nothing but rustling leaves, a bird squawking now and then, and the crunch of my sneakers on the gravel paths. They let me walk outside alone now. That's because I've kept my room clean and earned privileges, unlike some of the yahoos around here who can't control themselves. I like to cruise along the paths that wind through the elm trees and around the lagoon. At first I didn't go too far, not knowing where any of the paths led, but then Dr. Feelgood told me they all end up back at the Hospital. So I checked it out and he was right for once.

The lagoon is my favorite spot. These huge birds gather there, waddling on the shore or gliding alongside their reflections on the water. I asked Dr. Feelgood and he says they're geese. I never saw geese before, so what do I know? We only have pigeons at home, perched sort of nervously on the roof of our building. Anyway, these geese look disorganized as hell when they're on dry land, kind of milling around aimlessly and looking confused, but when they slide into the lagoon, they're transformed; it's like they're where they should be, where everything comes naturally and smoothly.

I've been here for three months and twelve days. Most of the time I don't mind it, but I worry about my mom living alone. She really doesn't have anybody to look after her but me. No man or anything. Don't get me wrong, she's had a few dates; she's pretty good-looking, for a mother. There were one or two guys she liked, I could tell, because she'd flutter around humming show tunes before they came by to pick her up. But after a few weeks they always disappeared. Then Mom would clean the apartment – scour the sinks, wash the walls, polish the furniture, in little stabbing strokes, with her hair pulled back and her lips pressed together. This one guy wasn't all that bad, either. He was from Milwaukee and once he even gave me a rookie card for Robin Yount. Mom's had no luck in the romance department. And she has no family to fall back on, either. Like me, she's an only child. When my mom was eleven years old, her mother dropped dead in a grocery store aisle holding a jar of gherkins. Something burst in her brain. I guess that makes my mom an orphan, now, thanks to me.

I've only seen Mom once since the day they brought me here from the Juvenile Detention Center. We sat in the day room, mostly alone except for some morons playing Hearts at the card table by the windows. She was okay at first, because I was here instead of jail. That was such a relief, she said. But then she got all weepy, and she tried to hug me. So I pushed her away. Boy, that really did it, let me tell you. She got red, and then she covered her face with her hands and started talking crazy through her fingers, like "I never wanted you to know . . ." and stuff like that. She blubbered some more but I just took off. I couldn't sit there for one more minute, you know? After that, Dr. Feelgood said maybe she shouldn't visit again for a while. Which is just fine with me.

I'm keeping this journal because Dr. Feelgood thinks it's a good idea. He says that sometimes stuff you didn't know you knew comes out when you're writing. He thinks I'm in a "netherworld," reality-wise. No kidding, that's how he talks. It doesn't make any sense to me, either. But I don't argue with his lame-brained theories. Around here, you've got to play along to get privileges, like in the beginning, when I wanted my belt and shoelaces back. I was sick and tired of shuffling around and hiking up my pants all the time. So I wised up – smiled at the nurses, joked around with the yahoos, even said a few words now and then to Dr. Feelgood – and it worked. I got my stuff back in record time.

My journal is private. Dr. Feelgood can't see it; no one can unless I say so. I know this is true because I slide this notebook under my mattress before I go to sleep at night. If anyone tried to take it, I'd wake up. I'm a light sleeper these days. The only person I show this to sometimes is Clarence, because he's cool and he offered to clean up my spelling. If I'm going to do this, I want to do it right.

Like when I killed Grandpa. I did that right. I made sure he was dead before I turned off the ignition on the car. Mom always told me that if I'm going to do something in life, I should do it the best that I can.

* * *

Clarence is a big, black dude who sweeps and mops up around here, usually at night. Sort of a janitor, I guess, except he also helps subdue patients when they freak out and that kind of thing. He told me he dropped out of school at sixteen because his mom needed help making ends meet. He and I have one big thing in common – he grew up without a father, too. But at least he knew who his father was – a blackjack dealer in Las Vegas named Marcel Brooks. Me, I never could get Mom to tell me squat about my father. My birth certificate, which I found once at the bottom of Mom's underwear drawer, just says "Father: *Unknown*." Clarence says it didn't make any difference, knowing his father's name, since they only met once anyway, that he can remember.

When he was nineteen, Clarence took a Greyhound bus to Vegas and tracked his father down at the Flamingo. He said his dad was a lot like the casino; they'd both seen better days. He introduced himself, and Marcel looked kind of scared at first. But they spent the night together, drinking scotch at the bar when his dad got off shift. Nothing heavy, just shooting the breeze and catching up on Clarence's entire childhood. Marcel told Clarence that he tried to leave the gambling world behind when he got married, but his job with the Department of

Transportation, scoring the written tests for driver's licenses, was too damn boring after the lights and hustle of dealing. So he asked his wife, Clarence's mother, to move back to Vegas with him but she said no. Too much temptation there, she said. So that's why he left when he did, even though Clarence was only a baby at the time. Clarence told his dad it was okay, he wasn't there to lay blame for the past, and then he left for the bus station.

That was always my dream: to find my father, and sit down with him and just talk for hours and hours. Maybe after that, we could go to a ball game, or he could take me to work with him and introduce me to all his buddies. I used to bug my mom about him all the time. But she would just say, "That's ancient history, Garson. Now go wash your hands for dinner." Or, "go clean your room," or "take out the garbage." Finally I gave up. Clarence was lucky, finding his father, even if it was only for one night.

I asked Clarence and he said it was okay for me to write about him, seeing as how no one sees this notebook except me. Even though he's a high school dropout, Clarence loves books and so he reads all the time when he's not working. He even lends me his books to read when he's finished them. To return the favor, I watch out for Clarence when he's sneaking a read in the janitor's closet. It's a pretty big closet at the end of the hall on the second floor. There's just one bare bulb hanging down with a string attached to the broken chain, but he's got a comfy armchair underneath and a wobbly little table for his coffee mug. Sometimes, when Clarence is off work, I write my journal in there.

I don't really belong here. For one thing, I'm younger than everyone else. Even Averell, who's fifteen, has a year on me. For another thing, I'm not crazy. I don't talk to myself like Averell, or wear earrings like Raymond, or get spacey like Justice Justice. I'm just a normal kid no one knew what to do with. So here I am.

* * *

When I slipped into the janitor's closet this morning to write in my journal, I could hear someone mumbling in the corner even before I pulled the string on the light chain. When the closet flooded with light Averell looked up at me over his shoulder, squinting in the glare. He was squatting and hunched over a cardboard shoebox. He raised one finger to his lips, so I shut the door.

"Whatchya doing?" I asked. Averell sidled sideways on his haunches and I peered over his shoulder into the box. A tiny brown bird sat very still inside, half-buried in tattered bits of newspaper. Just when I thought the bird might be dead, it chirped meekly and riffled its peach-fuzzy feathers. Averell stroked the bird's back with one finger. I bent down to get a better look.

"I found her under a tree down by the lagoon," said Averell. "She must have fallen out of her nest."

"So what's she doing here?"

"I'm going to save her," Averell said, raising his bruised eyes to mine. Averell didn't sleep much so he always looked like he had two fading shiners.

"Okay," I said, trying not to sound skeptical, "but why're you keeping her in the closet?"

"Don't tell Raymond," Averell whispered, which in a way answered my question. He continued to stroke the bird's back, cooing under his breath. "Don't worry, Baby. We won't let Raymond near you." It sounded more like a prayer than a promise.

"You gonna be long in here?" I said, straightening up. Averell stood as well, towering over me by a foot. Everything about him was thin and pale, from his peeling fingernails to his white-blond, flyaway hair. The slightest breeze – even the draft in the closet – sent his hair wafting in eighteen different directions. His weight rested mostly on one leg, his good leg, not the one he shattered jumping off the roof of his garage. He hugged his ribs for a second, still staring down at the box. His shirt cuffs had ridden up a bit, exposing the thin red scars on the white insides of his wrists.

"Keep an eye on her for me, okay Garson?" he said. Then he opened the door a crack to check the hall, and limped out. I plopped into the armchair to write this entry. Every once in a while Baby gives a small chirp. It's kind of sweet.

* * *

Of all the loony tunes in this joint, Raymond is probably the looniest. I think they hide him somewhere on visiting day because if the relatives of other patients got a load of Raymond, there'd be a mad rush of people hauling their sons and grandsons and nephews out of here. Besides, Raymond never seems to have any visitors. I've never even seen his parents, though he went home for a weekend visit once so I know they're around.

Raymond pretends he's Madonna. Not the Virgin Mary. The Material Girl; you know, the pop star and movie actress. It all started when Raymond learned that he and Madonna were born on the same day (of different years, obviously). He more or less decided they were soul mates after that. I tried to tell him that something like one in every 365 people on earth was born on that day. It doesn't mean a thing. If they were all soul mates, there'd be no wars or race riots or any of that stuff; we'd all be dancing around with flowers in our hair, holding hands like a bunch of idiots. But Raymond just smirked and shook his head.

Like a lot of her fans, he prefers Madonna's original look and ignores all the makeovers after that. So he wears a lot of large crosses around his neck. He also cuts all his shirts off short and lets his pants ride low to show off his navel. His hair is long and bleached blonde, and he shaves his black stubble like two or three times a day, and applies eyeliner like a professional model. His constant demands for more makeup and hair coloring have been ignored. I think Dr. Feelgood is hoping to wean Raymond off his Madonna obsession slowly. Meanwhile, Raymond's roots are looking darker every day.

Raymond bounded into the dayroom this morning with even more energy than usual. I was reading a book I borrowed from Clarence about these two kids in this prep school playing a game where they jump out of a big tree into a river even though it's very dangerous. Anyway, it was pretty interesting so I didn't notice Raymond at first, which is weird because Raymond is hard to miss, even in this joint. But he plopped into the chair next to mine and launched right in, even though I kept my eyes glued to the open book.

"I think Averell's got a secret," he said, pricking the ears of a few of the yahoos around us.

Naturally, I thought of Baby. So I said, without looking up, "You're imagining things, Raymond."

"I'm sure of it," he said. I peered at him out of the corner of my eye and saw him fingering a large silver cross hanging from a cord around his neck. His nails were painted purple. You could tell he took care of them, with manicures or whatever. They were nice.

"Based on what, exactly?"

"The whole shower thing." Averell refused to shower or dress in front of the rest of us. He picked odd hours to use the curtain-less shower stalls in the second floor bathroom while everyone else slept. I ran into him once at about three o'clock in the morning when he came into the bathroom with his shower stuff. I was taking a leak in the urinal. I tried to tell him I was almost done, but he'd already darted away.

"He's just shy," I said. Inwardly, I sighed with relief. Not Baby, after all.

"He's hiding something," Raymond said, "you'll see. There are no secrets here." He turned swiftly on Kyle, the yahoo who had edged closest to eavesdrop. "What's your problem?" Raymond said. "Never seen a celebrity before?" Kyle shrank back and returned to his checkers game. "Too scared to ask for an autograph," said Raymond, with a smug smile. He sank back in his chair, draping his arms over the armrests like a queen, fingers dripping over the edges. It looked like he planned to stay awhile, so I closed my book slowly and, with a fake yawn, stood to leave. I figured I should warn Averell that Raymond was gunning for him. And I had a pretty good idea of where to find Averell.

"See you later," I said, as casually as possible.

"Go," said Raymond, waving one hand lazily as if to shoo away a fly.

I ambled into the hall and then waited to see whether Raymond was wise to me. After a couple of minutes, the hall still empty, I ducked into the janitor's closet and eased the door shut. The closet was dark and felt empty, but I heard Baby's faint chirp while fumbling in the black for the light string. I gave the string a yank, squinted in the harsh light. The eyedropper on the table told me Averell had been there and gone.

I finally found him crouching behind the Hospital, his lean frame folded like a wire hanger, poking his fingers in the ground under some bushes. The warm breeze fluttered his hair, paler than ever in the sunlight. I squatted down next to him and watched while he tried to pull a slimy earthworm free from the ground, stretching it almost to the breaking point before it popped out and squirmed in the palm of his hand.

"Dinner for Baby?" I asked.

"Yeah." Averell let the worm slide off his tipped hand into a metal can by his feet. Inside, the worm wriggled among a few of its cousins.

"Listen, " I said, "Raymond thinks you've got some deep, dark secret because of, well, your . . . shower habits. So keep an eye out for him."

"It doesn't seem fair, does it?" Averell said, rocking back on his heels a bit. "This whole food chain business, I mean. Why should worms have to die for sparrows to live? It's barbaric, if you think about it." Averell poked at the ground half-heartedly. "The strong survive and the weak are just . . ."

"Shit out of luck?"

"Sacrificed," he said. A gust of wind sent his hair whipping.

I thought about it for a minute. "They do alright," I said, pointing to the tin can, "in the end."

"How do you figure?" Averell said.

"Well," I reminded him, "in the end, we're all worm food, right?"

Averell looked a little shocked. Then he almost smiled, but not quite.

To be honest, I wasn't much interested in the ethics of evolution. "Okay, Darwin," I said, pushing myself up, palms on knees. "I'll catch you later." I'd done what I could. Some guys you just can't help, they're so pathetic. I mean he's worried about worms, for God's sake.

* * *

I'm wiped out today from lack of sleep. Justice Justice called a case for trial last night, and I was supposed to be a witness. Usually I'll skip a trial if it sounds like a rinky-dink case.

I should explain about Justice Justice. His real name is Hubert Justice, and he's around a hundred years old. It just so happens that on the outside, he's an actual justice on the State Supreme Court. So everyone calls him Justice Justice. He's been a judge forever, or as far back as anyone can remember, because the ding-dong voters keep reelecting him, term after term. They do this even though he disappears for a month every few years on "sabbatical" so that he can recover from his latest nervous breakdown. The rumors fly but no one seems to care. It's like his name is destiny or something. Let's face it: you see that name on a ballot, and you're just going to mark it, you know?

The first time I saw Justice Justice he was shuffling around in his flannel bathrobe, his hair uncombed and his hands, covered with liver spots and bulging blue veins, trembling. Still, I figured he must be on the staff. Hooten Hospital is for teenage boys only. Finally, I pulled Raymond aside and pointed to the old man, saying, "What gives?" Raymond makes it his business to ferret out everyone's story around here. So he gave me the lowdown on Justice Justice. "He's tight with all the bigwigs in state government," said Raymond, "and pulls a lot of strings to get in here. Told me once he's afraid of the adult mental cases, scared they'll attack him in the shower or something. Plus, he likes Hooten – the town, I mean – it's small, no reporters, stuck in the middle of nowhere. He can hide out here. So he's been checking himself in and out for years." That was Raymond's take on the situation, but Clarence hinted there was a little more to it. Seems Hooten Hospital is constantly being cited by the State for some violation or another – things are pretty lax around here – but somehow, as long as Justice Justice keeps visiting, the doors of Hooten Hospital stay open. Go figure.

Anyway, Justice Justice thinks he's the greatest legal mind since Learned Hand (another judge with a name you just can't make up.) So he insists on meddling in the feuds that erupt now and then between the yahoos here. The stuff these guys fight about is petty as hell. Like last week, this bulimic dude named Norbert accused Kyle of stealing his toothbrush. And no one needs his toothbrush more than a bulimic. So we had this whole trial about it. Kyle was found guilty and sentenced to make Norbert's bed for a month but the sentence was never carried out on account of Norbert found his toothbrush the next morning under a towel in the corner of his room.

These trials aren't like the ones on TV. For one thing, there's no jury. The only possible jurors are the loons in here and Justice Justice doesn't think we're competent to pass judgment on each other. But he lets us ask questions sometimes. And we play our parts as witnesses and bailiffs and spectators. The spectators are there to hoot and holler in a stage whispery way so Justice Justice can bang the fake gavel he made by mangling a ping-pong paddle. Mostly though, the spectators doze or stare at the walls, or pick their noses or whatever. Of course, there are no lawyers. In the opinion of Justice Justice, the only people more useless than jurors are lawyers.

The case last night started out typically enough. Klepto Kyle was a bailiff, so he jostled my shoulder around 2:30 a.m. clutching a paper in his hand. Justice Justice had gotten hold of a prescription pad that Kyle filched from his shrink's office and was using it as subpoena paper because it was official-looking and had a lot of white space for him to scrawl on. Usually, the judge just scribbles his subpoenas on napkins or the backs of old envelopes.

"What's this?" I said, half-awake.

Kyle wafted the paper in front of my nose. "Rise and shine, Glinke. Your turn to testify tonight." Trials are always held in the middle of the night so the Hospital staff won't get wise and interfere.

"What about?"

"Madonna versus Moon." That really woke me up. Cases were named after the accuser and the accused. Raymond insisted that his "real" name be used, even though it's a first name and not even his own. Moon was Averell's last name.

"But what's it about?" I said, sitting up.

"Beats me. I'm just serving the subpoena." Kyle had the disgusting habit of spitting when he talked, so listening to this sentence was like walking through a sprinkler. He reached for the sheet covering me and ripped it back. "Let's go."

"Alright, alright," I said, "just spray your spit somewhere else, will you?" I got up and pulled on a sweater over my pajamas while Kyle eyeballed the personal stuff on my dresser. "Don't even think about it, Klepto," I said, and yanked on my socks. He balled his fists and shoved them into the pockets of his bathrobe.

We darted down the dimly lit hall, slid on our socks around the corner, and then hurried to the day room. When we got there I could tell right away that we were the last to arrive. All the main players were in their places: Justice Justice behind the heavy oak card table that he used as his makeshift bench, and Averell blinking beside him in an oversized armchair. He was blotchier than usual, and his normally wispy hair looked stringy, plastered to his head. Raymond, the accuser, stood facing both of them, his back to the audience. There were more spectators than usual, which struck me as a bad sign. Even Orville was there and he's what they call borderline catatonic. They had to prop him up on the couch with pillows.

Kyle took his place behind and to one side of the judge, with his legs spread and feet planted, hands behind his back. Justice Justice cleared his throat noisily, paused, swallowed the gunk he'd just brought up. Then he grasped his paddle and whacked it, with glancing blows, on the edge of the oak table three times. "Court will come to order," he said, his deep voice gravelly from ten thousand cigars. He dropped the gavel and leaned back in his chair. Thatches of white hair sprang from his skull and hooded his eyes like two old caterpillars. Underneath he had a droopy face and a spidery patchwork of broken veins around his nose. "Bailiff, call the case."

Kyle stepped forward and pretended to read from his prescription paper. "Madonna versus Moon." Then he stepped back and re-assumed the position he'd picked up, no doubt, from some old movie about Nazi Germany. I slipped into a chair on the edge of the spectators' gallery. "Opening statements begin with Mr., let's see, now . . .

Madonna," Justice Justice said with a nod toward Raymond.

Raymond stepped forward in his full Madonna getup. Long, dangly earrings pulled at his earlobes and his hair was teased and sprayed to give it more body. He wore his favorite pair of hip-huggers and a gauzy midriff blouse too sheer to hide the undergarment, a tired looking brassiere he'd smuggled into the Hospital after his one and only visit home. For some reason, he hadn't filled the cups with anything, so they just lay there all deflated and puckered on his chest. Silver crucifixes weighted all three of his necklaces and they clinked together as he stepped forward to speak.

"Thank you, your Honor." I really started to worry when I heard that. As a celebrity Raymond normally refused to show an ounce of respect for anyone else. Yet here he was, sucking up to Justice Justice, a demented old fart with a lucky name and a bad case of the shakes.

Raymond took a step closer to Averell, and then stopped to wrinkle his nose and flutter his hand before his face. The point was made. Someone tittered; everyone knew the nature of Raymond's complaint. Since my talk with him five days before, Averell had managed to avoid Raymond by skipping showers altogether. As his odor became more distinct, he was given more and more space by the rest of us. We'd heard through the grapevine that Averell's chart noted a sudden aversion to water, but the staff was tiptoeing around the problem, unsure how to react. Raymond didn't mince any words.

"He's ripe, Your Honor. It's offensive just to be in the same room with him." There was a murmur of support from the peanut gallery. Even Orville seemed to be bobbing his head, but that was just the ripple effect of another yahoo bouncing on the couch beside him.

"Yes, well, the Court will take judicial notice of the pungent aroma emanating from Mr. Moon," said Justice Justice. More titters earned the gallery a glare from His Honor under the arch of one white caterpillar.

Just then I happened to glance at the guy next to me and notice the square of paper pinned between his chubby fingers. I recognized the spiky loops in the ink strokes, like the readout from one of those EKG machines. "Hey, Timmy, you subpoenaed too?" I whispered. Timmy started, jerking his head – he's a nervous type – and stared at me wide-eyed for a second. Then he relaxed a bit and shrugged. "It's a forgery," he said. "Raymond and Kyle – they got hold of the prescription pad and subpoenaed everyone." He must have seen my confusion, because he shrugged again. "Who knows?" he said.

"So Mr. Moon," Justice Justice said, turning to Averell, "is it true that you have neglected to bathe for – "

"Five days," Raymond supplied.

" . . . yes, five days?" Justice Justice continued.

Averell sat with rounded shoulders, his hands clasped in his lap. "I don't see what business that is of anyone but me," he said mildly.

"Yes, well, perhaps you're right, but that will be for the Court to decide. Answer the question, young man." The Judge always sounded like a tire on ice, his words slipping, finding traction, surging ahead. "Has it been, let's see now, five days since you last showered?"

"Yes."

"I see. Okay, then, can you tell the Court why it is you refuse to shower?"

Averell scratched behind his ear. Raymond put his hands on his hips, and someone coughed in the back of the room.

"Speak up, young man. Why aren't you bathing?"

It only took a few more seconds of silence for Raymond to burst. "He's hiding something!"

Justice Justice rubbed the inside corners of his runny eyes. "So what relief are you requesting, Mr. Madonna? I can't forcibly compel the defendant to shower." That was the best thing about Justice Justice – he understood the limits of his authority.

"Just make him take off his shirt," said Raymond. Averell's head jerked up and he stared at Raymond in horror. "Look," Raymond said in a wheedling tone, "the guy's shy and probably embarrassed because he doesn't have chest hair or maybe there's a rash there or an extra nipple or whatever. The thing is, if he shows us once, then that will be that. He won't have to hide it anymore, and then he can take a shower like the rest of us."

"I'm not going to order a strip search, Raymond."

"Not a strip search, Judge. Just his shirt. That's no big deal – I'll even do it first. See?" And with that Raymond crossed his arms before him and pulled his filmy blouse off over his head. Someone groaned behind me. But as Raymond struggled to unhook the brassiere, thirty-odd sets of curious eyes were glued to his back. Abruptly giving up, Raymond peeled the bra straps off his shoulders and pushed down the brassiere so it hung around his hips, the straps drooping like abandoned suspenders.

"See Judge, it's nothing," he said, and twirled around with his hands in the air, his bra straps and those dangly earrings flying sideways.

This pitiful display seemed to impress Justice Justice, who turned to Averell.

"What of it, Mr. Moon. Care to pull up your shirt for us?"

Averell looked frozen. I willed him to at least shake his head, but he just sat there, not even blinking.

Raymond saw his chance. "C'mon Kyle, you heard the Judge." In a move that looked pre-arranged, Kyle and Raymond grabbed Averell and pulled him from his chair. Averell raised his hands to ward them off but hugged his elbows to his ribcage. His attackers yanked at his shirt, ripped one sleeve. With a small shriek, Averell twisted and squirmed away from their hands. A few spectators gasped, but we were rooted to our chairs.

"Now wait just a . . . ," Justice Justice began, and then raising his voice, "I haven't issued any order yet . . . "

Averell flailed, his face contorted and shiny with oily sweat. Kyle managed to pin Averell's arms behind his back while Raymond tried to tear his shirt open. A button popped free. I scrambled over the empty chair in front of me and leapt toward Raymond's back just as Averell's shirt ripped to expose the center of his smooth pale chest. I tackled Raymond and we both slammed into the hardwood floor. Above us I heard Averell whimpering and three sharp raps of the judge's paddle. I could see Averell's legs go limp but Kyle must have held him up from behind. Then we rolled and Raymond was sitting on my stomach, pressing my wrists to the floor. He was breathing hard, one earring gone; his fingernails dug into my flesh. The three crucifixes hung straight down, almost touching my chin. I felt a rush in my ears and there was a bitter taste in the back of my throat.

A booming voice pierced the din. "Just what the hell is going on here?" Clarence loomed in the doorway, his broad forehead plowed in furrows. Raymond and I stopped struggling and the room became eerily quiet. I felt the pressure lift from my wrists. The only sound was some panting and a small bleating sound from Averell. Then someone said, "Holy shit, look at that." And we all looked at Averell, still propped up from behind like a scarecrow. His eyes were downcast and a little string of snot hung from his nose. His shirt was hanging open, partly ripped away.

All the way down the left side of his torso, from his armpit to his hipbone, snaked a jagged purple scar. It was nothing like the wimpy scratches on his wrists. It was thick and puckered and it looked like it had been there for a long time.

Still trapped on my back, I watched Raymond stare at the scar sort of glassy-eyed. Kyle picked that moment to let go of Averell, who slipped to the ground in a crumpled pile. Then Clarence was there, lifting Averell gently by the shoulders and pulling his tattered shirt closed as best he could. "You all get to bed now, you hear me?" he growled. And we did, without another word.

* * *

Clarence told me that the Hospital administrators knew all along about our night court sessions. After talking it over, the shrinks had decided it might be good – therapeutic, they call it – for us to work out our own differences. After the attack on Averell, they changed their minds. Justice Justice was finally, and for the first time in his career, voted off the bench.

Everyone involved in the fiasco lost privileges, except Averell, of course, who spent two days resting in the infirmary with a sprained wrist. So I'm stuck inside the Hospital again. No more walks on the grounds for a month. Oh, and Orville also escaped punishment, mostly because he didn't know what was going on, but also because, let's face it, there's nothing more they can take away from him. I mean the guy's practically a vegetable.

Averell was released from the infirmary yesterday. I watched for him in the cafeteria and the day room all morning but he didn't show. Finally I went to his room and knocked softly on his door. I thought I heard a faint "Come in" so I pushed the door open and entered. Averell was sitting on his neatly made bed, staring out the window at the trees that guarded the lagoon. I stood there until he turned and looked up at me. His eyes were more bruised than ever.

"I took care of Baby while you were gone," I said. I didn't tell him that without ground privileges, I had to bribe Harvey to dig up the worms. It cost me two marbles and my Robin Yount rookie card.

"She'll die anyway," was all he said.

There was this long uncomfortable silence. "Raymond's lost all his privileges," I said. "They even took away his makeup and the bra he stole from his mother." Averell just blinked at the window. "Boy, is he pissed," I said, babbling a little now. "Mostly at Clarence, for reporting us. And me, of course. For the sucker-jump. He broke two nails." Averell turned and smiled at me, sort of, and I found myself thinking that the smile was terrible. It would have been better, somehow, if he had burst into tears or screamed or something.

After that smile I left.

Back in the day room, Raymond had commandeered a card table normally used for Sheepshead and conned the suckers sitting there into playing Poker. Naturally, Raymond was dealing, so he had control over the game and its consequences. One of the players was Harvey. That made me a little nervous. Harvey is fat and flabby; he chews his nails and wears his hair in a crew cut. He looks like the guy who breaks down and cries on the first day of basic training. I had sworn Harvey to secrecy, but Raymond could pry a confession out of a priest.

So I hung around the table for a while. Pointing to the chips I asked, "Whatchya playing for today?" The chips were always stand-ins for something else that, judging from the messy pile in front of Raymond, he would collect.

Raymond smiled. "Secrets and favors." He started dealing the next hand of five-card stud so I took a chance and shot Harvey a hard look. Harvey looked down and picked up his first card with chubby fingers. He had only a few chips left. Harvey knew about the worms, but I hadn't been foolish enough to tell him about Baby. Still, the worms would be enough to get Raymond going on a slow day. I decided to stick around until the morons finished their game. I laid down on a couch close by, trying to seem casual about it. The couch sagged so badly it felt more like a hammock, but it was within earshot of the game.

It didn't take Raymond long to clean them all out. He probably cheated. Anyhow, a half hour later, he was collecting his winnings. He started with Harvey, and I was glad I'd stayed in the neighborhood.

"What's it going to be, Harvey," Raymond said, "favor or secret?" What a sweet guy — he was giving them a choice.

I sat up and bored a hole in Harvey's forehead with my eyes. He glanced at me quickly and mumbled, "Favor."

"Okay," said Raymond, "I'll get back to you later. Rufus, what about you?"

"Secret," Rufus said.

"Who about?" Raymond asked, like he didn't believe Rufus already.

"Clarence," said Rufus. I had just begun to relax, sinking back into the couch cushions, when I heard that. I sat up again.

"What about him?" said Raymond.

Rufus bent forward, his chin almost touching the tabletop, and lowered his voice. Everyone leaned in.

"He be an ex-con." There was a hush around the table.

"Says who?" said Raymond.

"My Uncle Reggie. He come and visit me bout a month ago. And he seen Clarence, pushin' his mop. And he say to me, I know that man. I done time with that man, in Alabama, twenty-some year ago. So I say, you sure? And he say to me, real sad-like, he say some things don't nobody forget." Rufus leaned back and crossed his arms, satisfied he'd paid his debt in full. And from the look on Raymond's face, I could tell that he had. With interest.

"Well, well, well," said Raymond. I stayed on the couch, just thinking, until Raymond finished his business with the morons. Then I left to find Justice Justice.

* * *

Averell finally left his room today. He was already in the day room when I wandered in after breakfast. I sat down near him, facing the windows, leaving one empty chair between us. I propped my feet up on the cover of the cold radiator and closed my eyes to bask in the morning sun that poured through the windowpanes. We sat there like that for a few minutes, like we were on the deck of a cruise ship or something.

"Some day," Averell said, "I'm going to open one of these windows and Baby's going to fly right out of here."

I didn't bother to point out that the windows were hermetically sealed. The Hospital didn't want anyone flying out of them, I guess.

"Where will she go?" I asked instead.

"To her family, of course. They'll all reunite at the lagoon."

It was a nice image. I was real relaxed, with my eyes closed and the sun glowing behind my eyelids while I watched Baby soar over the lagoon with her siblings.

Then Averell had to ruin it.

"What was he like, Garson? Your grandfather?"

"I don't know," I said, frowning a little. "I only knew him for two weeks."

"Two weeks?"

"He lived in Wisconsin, but we never visited him or anything. Mom didn't want to. Then he just showed up one day at my school, outside the playground. Standing behind the fence. And he told me who he was. So we hung out together, for a while."

"Was he nice?"

I shrugged. "He was okay, I guess." My heart fluttered. "He took me to the racetrack, once."

"Oh yeah?"

"Yeah." I closed my eyes again. "There was a big crowd there and it was sunny, sitting in the stands. Grandpa sneaked me a beer and I kept it between my feet. The best part, though, was the horses. They were . . . magnificent." I blushed a little; 'magnificent' is such a fruity word, like something a snooty girl would say. "Grandpa placed bets for me, two bucks on every race. Taught me how to read the racing form. Look at the track, the jockey, all that. Not that dumb stuff like the name of the horse or the color the jockey wears. I won eight bucks."

Averell seemed to expect something more, or maybe I was just nervous.

"The best part is when the gun goes off, at the start of the race," I said. "There's this moment, when the gates open, and you expect the horses to spring right out. But they don't, not right away. There's this split second when nothing moves. Everything seems frozen. And your heart just stops. Then suddenly, there they are, pounding down the track." I looked sidelong at Averell. "It's kind of hard to explain," I said lamely. Averell just sat there. We were quiet for a while, just resting our feet on the radiator.

I thought maybe he'd let it go.

"Why'd you do it, Garson?" he asked dreamily. "You've never said."

"Huh?"

"Why'd you kill your grandfather?"

He wasn't the first to ask. In this place everyone knows your history, to some extent. But usually I'm ready with some joke, some putdown, to shut them up. Averell caught me off-guard. So I did something I've never done before.

I answered the question honestly. I told him the truth.

"I don't know."

(Sorry, Dr. Feelgood. I guess this journal won't be as useful as you'd hoped.)

* * *

It took Justice Justice nearly a week to do his research. Since he's a judge, and staying here of his own free will, they allow him a special privilege: visits to a law library. Unfortunately, the only good one nearby is located inside a maximum-security prison about forty miles from the Hospital. So Justice Justice doesn't exercise the privilege too often. He went yesterday as a favor to me, after I laid a heavy guilt trip on him for losing control of Averell's trial.

He caught up to me in the cafeteria line this morning. Even though Raymond was half a room away, his spies could be anywhere, so I hushed the old man and told him to meet me by the janitor's closet after breakfast. Then I remembered my counseling session with Dr. Feelgood. "Make it noon," I said, "and act natural, for God's sake." Justice Justice was so obvious, whispering in my ear and darting jerky glances around the room. I broke away from him and sat down next to Harvey, who chewed and slurped with his mouth open, so that no one at his table dared to start a conversation.

My counseling session was a bust, as usual. Dr. Feelgood talks a lot because I don't say much. His voice is soothing and low, like the sound of the road rumbling beneath you during a long car trip. Usually I sit on the suede couch with all the creases in it, and he takes this straight-backed wooden chair kitty-corner from me. I always spend my time looking around his office at his nicked up desk, the rows and rows of boring-looking books tipped at odd angles on the shelves, the ratty old Oriental rug at my feet with half the fringe missing. He always asks about the trial. It's like he's the dentist probing a rotten tooth, and I'm sitting there shot full of Novocain. Mostly I watch the dust motes floating by his window.

Today he gave me some bound papers and asked me to read them before our next session on Friday. I peered at the first page through the clear plastic cover. "It's the transcript of your trial," Dr. Feelgood explained. "That is, part of the trial. Your mother's testimony." The skin between his eyes puckered.

"I was there," I said.

"Do you remember what was said?"

"Sort of," I lied. I didn't listen during the trial. It was boring.

"Read it again," he said carefully. "We'll talk about it Friday."

And then the strangest thing happened. I saw a drop fall on the transcript cover, and then another one, and I swear to God I almost looked up at the ceiling to check for a leak because I didn't know where the drops were coming from. And then I felt this streaking on my cheeks and it sort of hit me that I was crying. Don't ask me why. I wasn't feeling sad or anything at all, really. But these stupid tears just started plopping and I couldn't stop them for some reason. Everything was blurry but I felt Dr. Feelgood's big smooth hand on mine and I just snatched mine away. It was like a reflex; I didn't think about it. And then he says to me, "Garson, it'll be okay."

When he finally let me go, I had to hustle to make my appointment with Justice Justice. But when I reached the hallway it was empty. I waited for a couple minutes, pacing back and forth with the transcript pressed to my chest. Finally I thought to check the closet. Sure enough, Justice Justice was relaxing in Clarence's chair, his eyelids drooping like the rest of his face. I slammed the door shut behind me and the old man's eyes flew open. Then he half closed them again.

"There's a bird in here," he said.

"Yeah, well don't mention it to Raymond, okay?" I dropped the transcript on the table, which listed to one side. Unfortunately, this grabbed the attention of Justice Justice. He knew a legal document when he saw one, and the case caption was easy to see through the plastic.

"What's this?" he asked, scooping up the transcript. It quivered in his hand until he let it fall into his lap.

"None of your beeswax," I said. It was such a babyish expression that I cringed a little. Justice Justice was paging through the document, wetting his shaky fingertip on his tongue between pages.

"Testimony of Hyacinth Glinke," he said. "Your mother, I presume?"

I nodded. "Dr. Feelgood is making me read it."

The old man's eyes seemed to devour the words printed on the page at his knees. He tried to rub his chin in a serious way but the twitching hand just made him look feeble. "You know, Garson, I could read this for you, if you wish," he said. "Interpret it. Summarize it. Save you the trouble."

My muscles all seemed to relax at once. In the corner, Baby chirped hopefully. "Would you?" I asked. "That would really help me out. But I need it by Friday."

"It shall be done," said Justice Justice, rather grandly. He leaned forward, covering the transcript with his forearms as if to hide it. "Now, shall we get to the business at hand?"

"Did you find out anything?"

"Oh my yes. Our Clarence has quite a history."

"Tell me."

"Well, let's see. It seems that Clarence was incarcerated in the Alabama state prison system for a number of years. He was convicted in 1964 of raping a white woman."

I felt the blood rush to my face. There had to be some kind of mistake. Justice Justice must have read my mind, because he went on in a hurry.

"The conviction was suspect, as it turned out. Well, that's putting it charitably. Years later, another convict confessed to the crime, and then it all came out. Subornation of perjury. Manufactured evidence. Prosecutorial misconduct. Quite a mess. Anyway, the Governor commuted his sentence, and Clarence walked free."

"He was, like, cleared?" I said, groping for the right word.

"Well, no, not officially. Technically, he *is* a convicted felon. But if you read the appellate decision, well – " and here the old man spread his hands like a preacher – "it's quite clear he was wrongly convicted. Railroaded, if you will."

"Did he get a new trial?"

"No. He never did. The Governor stepped in, quite conveniently for everyone involved. He commuted Clarence's sentence to time served and a new trial became unnecessary."

"How long was Clarence in prison?"

"Sixteen years."

* * *

Averell is taking care of Baby again, with a vengeance. He is constantly feeding her worms, or dripping water into her outstretched beak with the eyedropper, or smuggling her outside for fresh air. She doesn't fly yet, but Averell believes that she will. He likes to take her to the lagoon, hoping she'll find her family there. So far, though, she's just hopped around on the grass, fluttering her wings a little. Or so Averell tells me. I can't go outside yet. If she does fly away one day, I hope I'm there to see it.

Dr. Feelgood was mad at me at our Friday session. He tried to hide it but I could tell by the way he took off his glasses and rubbed the bridge of his nose. Not that I give a crap. Why should I spill my guts to that quack, anyway? He'll just use it against me. And then I'll never get out of this place.

It was all Justice Justice's fault. He promised me he'd read my transcript. I figured he'd give me the highlights, or at least enough to fake my way through a counseling session. But when I asked him about it Thursday night, he looked a little lost. He'd forgotten all about it. That happens a lot with Justice Justice. He stuttered something about "the press of other business" but I could tell it was just an excuse. The old fart couldn't even find my transcript.

So the counseling session shouldn't be a total waste I tried to pump Dr. Feelgood for information on Clarence, who hasn't worked a shift since Raymond's poker game. I was pretty subtle about it. I asked whether Clarence would be going on our field trip next month to the natural history museum. (All the patients and staff usually go.) But my ploy didn't work. Dr. Feelgood just told me to stop changing the subject – the subject, of course, being me. He gave me another transcript and suggested we read it together, with me being the prosecutor and him being my mother. I said no thanks. Our session ended thirty-five minutes early, which was just fine with me.

I still have the new transcript he gave me. I still haven't read it.

* * *

Clarence lumbered into the day room today just as the afternoon shift was starting. I was so happy to see him that I practically leapt out of my chair. It was a good thing I had to untangle my crossed legs first, or I might not have noticed Raymond's reaction.

Raymond's face drained and all the cards he was holding just slipped, one by one, out of his fingers. Clarence surveyed the room but he didn't dwell on Raymond. Then, just before he turned to leave, Clarence gave me a little wink. I didn't want to follow him with Raymond watching, so I sat tight for a while. Raymond abandoned his game and stood for a long time brooding by the windows. It was the most subdued I'd ever seen him.

I caught up with Clarence later in the janitor's closet. I was bursting with questions when I slipped in, but once inside, a shyness came over me. Even though Clarence and I had shared a lot of personal stuff, I didn't feel right knowing something about him that he didn't know I knew.

"You're here," I said.

He smiled. "That I am."

I looked down and scuffed one toe of a sneaker with the other. "I thought maybe you got fired."

Clarence laughed from deep in his throat. "By all rights, I should've been."

"You really think so?"

"Well son, I did lie on my application, years ago, when I first came to work here."

"You did?" I asked, playing dumb.

"Something tells me you know what I lied about."

We were quiet for a minute. Even Baby kept her thoughts to herself, or maybe she was just sleeping.

"I'm not saying it was a right thing," Clarence said, "but I needed a job. And most places don't hire convicted felons."

"But if Dr. Feelgood finds out – "

"He already knows."

I stared at him, stunned.

"He's not the ignoramus you take him for, Garson."

"But . . ."

"Turns out Dr. Fielgud knew all along. From the very beginning, my first interview with the man. My manner gave me away. He saw the signs of long-term incarceration. The way I walked, the way I talked, the way I asked his permission to use the toilet."

I was still sputtering, so Clarence spelled it out for me.

"He hired me anyway. And never said a word about it, not to anyone. Not even to me." Clarence shook his big head in wonderment.

"So he's not going to fire you?"

"Nope. He called me just the other night, to let me know there was a rumor going around. We had a good long talk. And he said, Clarence, you've got a job here as long as you want it."

Every once in a while, your world shifts a little, and you're forced to see it differently than you did before. Coming face to face with the truth like that, no matter how right it feels, still sends you reeling at first. I was seeing Dr. Feelgood in a whole new way and it was making me a little bit sick.

* * *

Averell is frantic. In the cafeteria this morning, he caught me by the arm and jerked so hard I nearly dropped my tray. But my irritation vanished when I saw how fast his eyes were blinking. He started hopping on his good foot like he had to use the bathroom, but it was just nerves. Even his hair looked charged with static electricity.

"She's gone," he said.

Baby is missing.

We split up and spent all morning scouring the Hospital, looking everywhere for her. I checked most of the patient rooms while Averell searched the lobby and basement. We usually need permission to leave the second floor, but Averell sneaks around pretty well for a guy with a bum leg. The day room got a quick once-over because Raymond was prancing around in there like he was entertaining the troops or something. After that I ducked into room after room, acting all nonchalant if someone was in there, like it was just a friendly visit. But I didn't find so much as a feather.

At noon Averell and I huddled in the janitor's closet to decide our next move. By then Averell was convinced that Raymond was the culprit. Averell figured that Raymond had abducted poor Baby for ransom and the sooner we confronted Raymond, the better Baby's chances for survival. I don't think he thought Raymond would hurt Baby, just that she might die of neglect if she spent too much time in Raymond's clutches. By this time Averell was a nervous wreck. To tell the truth, I was pretty worried myself.

We didn't have to look far for Raymond. He was in his room after lunch, painting his nails neon pink. When we charged in, he was just screwing the cap back on his nail polish, fingers splayed to avoid smudging the wet lacquer. He didn't even look up.

"Don't you jerks know how to knock?" he said.

Averell looked stricken, all his nervous tics gone. So we shouldn't look like complete morons, I took the lead.

"We gotta talk to you."

"Yeah, well I'm kind of busy, so make it quick." Raymond sounded bored. He started waving his fingers in the air to dry his nails.

"Where's Baby?" Averell demanded, finding his voice. "What have you done with her?"

"Say what?" said Raymond. His hands stilled, suspended mid-wave.

"Give her back to me," said Averell.

Raymond's eyes narrowed to slits, and very slowly, he started waving his hands again. "I don't know what you're talking about." But it sounded weak, like he wasn't really trying to convince us.

"You can't take care of a bird, Raymond. She needs . . . special care. She's not that strong yet."

"A bird," said Raymond slowly. Then he looked at me and grinned. "So that's what the worms were for." That Harvey is such a wuss.

"You gotta give her back," said Averell. "C'mon, Raymond, please."

Raymond started blowing on his nails. Between hands, he says, real low-key, "What's it worth to you?"

"What do you want?" said Averell eagerly.

"He's lying, Averell," I said. It just popped out.

"Secret or favor?" Averell said. He was desperate, and it showed.

"Both," said Raymond, smiling now. "A modest favor, and a big secret. What do you say?"

I caught Averell's arm. "Don't do it."

"Just tell me what you want." Averell shrugged off my hand.

"To see your scar again," said Raymond. "That's the favor."

Before I could say a word, Averell had hiked his shirt up his left side. The puckered purple snake emerged, looking as lethal as ever.

"Now the secret," Raymond said matter-of-factly. "Tell me what crazy suicide attempt got you *that* one."

Averell teetered for a moment, one hand clutching his bunched shirttail near his left armpit. All the blood in his body seemed to have settled in that long angry scar. Raymond began to waft his hands again, as if to say, this is just another boring conversation and I can dry my nails while I listen.

"Don't trust him, Averell," I said. "Can't you see he's lying?"

"Shut up," he replied.

"Tell Madonna everything, honey," said Raymond.

Averell's face was gray but he opened his lips and the words came out, softly and haltingly and reluctantly, like refugee children tiptoeing across a minefield.

"It's from an operation," he said, "when I was little."

"What kind of operation?"

"It's kind of hard to explain."

"Well what did they do, remove all your internal organs?" Raymond said, pointing a neon pink nail at the scar. Averell still had his shirt up, like his torso was the visual aid for a high school speech.

"No . . . I . . . I got all the organs . . ."

"What's that supposed to mean?" said Raymond, exasperated.

"Well, only one heart was strong enough, see? No one realized that at first. When they did the operation, I was the one . . . and he . . ."

"Who?"

"Evan. My brother."

"What brother? You never mentioned a brother."

At that point Averell's voice went from anguished to utterly resigned. "The doctors said I was stronger than Evan. They said it was the right medical decision. The only real choice they had. But after the operation, my parents sued them anyway."

"I don't get it," Raymond said.

Averell took a deep breath. "They kept us together as long as they could, see? Until we both got too weak and sick, and the doctors said we would both die unless we were separated. But the operation didn't go right and halfway through my parents had to choose. One could live, or we both could die."

"And your parents chose you?"

Averell hesitated. Then ever so slightly, shook his head.

That's when he fainted. I instinctively grabbed at Averell's shirt, which did little more than soften his landing. Crouching beside him, I yelled his name a couple times, and within seconds he was blinking and touching his forehead. "Baby," he whispered. I turned to face Raymond, knowing it was pointless.

"What about it, Raymond. You got your dirt. Now where's the bird?"

"Beats me," said Raymond blandly, hiking his shoulders. I knew he was finally telling the truth. But I was haunted by the futility of Averell's confession. And it was like that, you know. It was like he was confessing to murder or something. I sprang up and grabbed Raymond by the collar.

"Listen, you freak," I hissed, like the snake on Averell's body come to life. "You better find that bird fast."

"Be careful, will you?" said Raymond. "My nails are still wet."

* * *

Averell leaned on me a little as we walked back to his room. He was still pretty shaky. While he sat on his bed staring out toward the tree-lined lagoon, I paced the room, trying to explain to him that we'd been fooled.

Raymond didn't know a thing. But Averell was listening on another frequency, it seemed. He was clinging to his original theory.

"She must be dead," he said. His voice was flat and sounded far away. "Otherwise he would have given her back to me."

"I don't think so, Averell. He just played us, is all."

Averell continued to stare out the window. His hands lay limp on the bedspread. They looked broken, useless. "Stay away from me, Garson," he said. It was so soft I wasn't sure if I had heard him right.

"We should keep looking," I said. Averell just sat there, like he'd stopped listening. So after a while, I left him alone. I figured I'd find Baby somewhere, in some yahoo's closet, and bring her back to Averell safe and sound. Then we'd be okay again, like those geese skimming the surface of the lagoon.

By dusk I was exhausted, mostly from dodging the nurses and orderlies who were milling around the basement and first floor during the shift change. No one stopped me though. Sometimes chaos is your best cover. I didn't find any sign of Baby in the kitchen or the cafeteria or the room where they keep extra blankets and stuff. I even sneaked through the lobby while they were busy at the nurses' station preparing meds, their starched backs to me as I crept, crouched down, past the counter. I saw lots of stuff I never noticed before, like scuff marks on the linoleum and dust balls under the furniture. But no Baby. So I finally gave up and went back to my room. I'm going to bed early tonight. It's been a long day.

* * *

Ordinarily, he's the last guy I would have turned to. But for some reason, I ran straight to his door. I was dripping wet, shivering like a drunk in detox. I started pounding on the door and didn't stop until it swung open. Dr. Feelgood took one look at me and grabbed my shoulders. Then he pulled me to his chest.

"What is it?" Dr. Feelgood asked. "What's happened?" I was crying too hard to answer. He held one hand on the back of my head, over my wet hair, while his other arm braced my heaving shoulders. I gasped for a breath, again and again. Dr. Feelgood waited until my gasping slowed down. Then he pushed me back gently and said, "Tell me what's going on."

"It's Averell," I sputtered. "He's in the lagoon." And then my tears stopped, just like that. A cold, hard feeling began in the pit of my stomach and spread to my fingers and toes. Within seconds, I was a stone.

"Oh, God," said Dr. Feelgood.

Later, when the police arrived to question me, I told them part of the story. The part they were interested in. How I woke up late this morning and spent a lazy Sunday doing nothing. How I finally stopped at Averell's room to check on him because I hadn't seen him all weekend. How I'd stood in his room for a minute, worried by its emptiness, looking out his window at the trees hiding the lagoon. How it hit me, then, that Averell was there. At the lagoon. How did you know that, they asked suspiciously. I just knew, that's all. I can't explain it.

I ran down to the lagoon without thinking about what I'd find there. As I passed under an umbrella of leaves heading toward the shoreline, the first thing I saw were the geese, floating and skimming on the surface of the lagoon. Then I saw a gray shirt, the arms outstretched, swelling on the water. I leapt into the warm lagoon and slogged a few steps up to my knees. Startled by the splash, the geese spread their wings and lifted off the pond toward the opposite shore. My shoes filled with water, felt like anchors, and the water fought my legs like a nightmare. I belly flopped onto the surface and pumped my arms, frantically, snorting water. Then I was next to the ballooning shirt. I saw tendrils of hair floating like seaweed just below the surface. It was Averell, face down in the middle of the lagoon.

I stopped then, bicycling with my heavy feet to keep my chin above water. Averell bobbed in the waves I was making. The tip of his ear broke the surface and submerged again. It was blue. He looked so peaceful that I knew he was dead. I couldn't bring myself to touch him. My nose sank under water, and I struggled to find the air. In a moment of panic, I turned my back on Averell and swam sloppily to the shore. The lagoon pulled at me as I dragged myself up the bank, soaked clothes clinging to my calves and forearms, water dripping down my face. And then I ran, clumsily, through the trees, back to the Hospital, to Dr. Feelgood.

I found out later that the Hospital staff knew Averell was missing but didn't want to worry the other patients. They had searched all weekend without ever thinking to check the lagoon.

I keep seeing that gray shirt. It was the same one I grabbed trying to break Averell's fall when he fainted on Friday in Raymond's room. I didn't tell the police about that, or about Baby either. I plan to take care of Raymond myself.

* * *

By midnight we were all in the day room. It was like old times. Justice Justice couldn't find his ping-pong gavel, but someone gave him a hammer to use instead. It was a heavy industrial hammer that a workman had left behind after installing shelves in one of the rooms. Justice Justice had trouble lifting it and it wobbled dangerously in his hand. His customary three strikes on the oak table left three overlapping grooves the size of quarters on the tabletop.

I took a play out of Raymond's book and persuaded Kyle to subpoena everyone. The spectators looked a little edgy, knowing that this trial was forbidden. Except Orville, of course. He just leaned on the couch pillows, drooling up a storm.

Justice Justice called us to order. Raymond was draped in the witness chair, but he looked strange to me. The dark rings under his eyes reminded me of Averell. Then it hit me, why he looked so different. There were no bangles or bandanna, no eyeliner or lipstick, no hip-huggers or sparkly sandals. Raymond looked almost like a normal guy, sitting there in his cotton pajamas. He had even wiped off his nail polish.

"Okay, let's see, Mr. Glinke," said Justice Justice, "we are gathered here at your behest. What is the nature of your complaint?" I had purposely kept Justice Justice in the dark. He was so anxious to play judge again that he didn't ask too many questions.

I pointed at Raymond's forehead. "He's a murderer." I heard rustling behind me from the crowd of yahoos. "He's actually a *double* murderer," I said, figuring I was on a roll.

"Well, Mr. Glinke," Justice Justice began, shaking his head a bit, "that is a rather serious charge. Just who were the victims of these alleged crimes?"

"Averell Moon and Baby."

"Averell had a baby?" Justice Justice was confused, as usual.

"No," I said, fumbling to explain, "Baby was a brown sparrow that Averell found at the lagoon. He was keeping her in the janitor's closet until she could fly. Raymond kidnapped her and killed her and that's why Averell . . . died like he did."

"Come now," said Justice Justice, "we are all aware of the unfortunate circumstances of Averell's passing. We all know that he committed – "

"Raymond killed him!" I said.

Raymond stiffened. That's when it struck me, I guess: how vulnerable he looked without makeup and jewelry and all that other jazz. Like a knight stripped of his armor. "Averell killed himself," Raymond said, dully. "And I never touched his stupid bird. I never even knew he had a bird until you two started spouting off about it."

Dimly, in some murky corner of my mind, I knew he was right. But there was a deeper truth than the one he was telling, and in the realm of that truth, Raymond was guilty as hell.

"It was your fault," I said.

Raymond, his face pink under a stubble of beard, rose from his chair. "You're the only murderer here," he said.

Maybe I should have seen that coming. But for some reason it never occurred to me that Raymond would use my history to turn the tables. It was such an obvious ploy. My scalp prickled like it was catching on fire.

"I was found not guilty."

"Yeah, by reason of insanity. That means you did it, moron."

"Temporary insanity. I'm fine now."

Justice Justice cleared his throat like only a cigar smoker can. "I think we're getting off the – "

"You're deluded," Raymond said. He sat down again, crossed his legs.

He wasn't making any sense. "What do you know about it?" I said.

"Oh, I know it all." An arrogant smile warped his face. He glanced toward Justice Justice. "You shouldn't leave things lying around where Karl can find them. They might fall into the wrong hands." Then he turned back to me. "Your mother tells a sad story."

He had the transcript. The shock was like plunging into icy water. I sucked in my breath to brace myself, like one of those nuts who hurl themselves into frigid Lake Michigan on New Years Day. Then I went numb all over. Raymond blurred, but I could still see his white teeth.

"She wasn't a bit sorry you killed her father. She hated her old man."

"Why?" The voice sounded weirdly like mine.

Raymond's teeth disappeared. "You know why, Garson."

There was a long expectant silence. I wanted to leave but my limbs wouldn't move. Gradually, Raymond came back into focus. He wasn't smiling anymore.

"She talked all about it at your trial," he said finally. "How he kept her like a prisoner, locked in the house. Home schooling, he told people, but just to keep them away." Raymond leaned forward, looking almost earnest. "She finally ran away, when she was fifteen. To Chicago. You know why, Garson, don't you?"

"To find a job," I said, hoping to shut him up.

"To save her baby. To keep him away from you. And she did, too, until he tracked you down."

By this time I had recovered my senses enough to make an escape. But we had a big audience and I didn't want Raymond spreading stories about my mother. My instincts were right, too, because Raymond wasn't done.

"She denied it," he said, "but I think your mom must've told you to kill him." Wow, that really did it. No way was I going to let a whopper like that go.

"She didn't even know that he found us," I said angrily. "He told me to keep it a secret."

"Then why did she need protection? Your mom said she thought you were trying to protect her."

I didn't know how to answer his question but I had to refute Raymond's theory somehow. So I just started talking about that day in the car. "We were driving toward the building where I live," I said, my voice sounding strangled, "and he said that he wanted to surprise my mom when she got home from work. He said I should let him in with my key and go to the movies, so he and my mom could catch up." I swallowed hard. Somehow I had to make Raymond understand my reasons for what I did that day. But it was hard to explain because I didn't understand it myself.

"He was driving along, flicking his ashes out the window," I continued, "and he was telling me about my mother, about what a comfort she was to him after his wife died. Then he started pounding on the steering wheel. And he said . . . he said my mother abandoned him when he needed her most. That she hid me from him, all these years. Deprived him of his own children."

I stopped talking. In my mind I was back in that car, thinking *You mean child, not children. Mom is an only child.* It's funny how little mistakes like that can really bug me. But it was none of Raymond's business and it didn't matter anyway. It was just something dumb I had thought at the time.

But Raymond wouldn't give up. "That doesn't explain anything," he prodded. "You had no reason unless your mom told you to do it."

"It wasn't thought out," I insisted. "We stopped at this gas station and Grandpa got out to buy cigarettes. He left the car running. I just sat there for maybe five minutes. I wasn't thinking about anything, really, except that I didn't want to take him to the apartment, or let him in with my key, or go to the movies."

Raymond just kept staring at me, waiting for more. I averted my eyes to look toward the window.

"So I slid over to the driver's seat. Grandpa came out and walked in front of the car. I shifted to drive and hit the gas. Ran him over. He was on the ground but I could hear him groaning. So I switched to reverse. Backed over him. Shifted to drive and went over him again. After that I stopped because I was pretty sure that he was dead." I paused and drew a deep breath. "I got out of the car, just to be sure. Walked to the back to check. He was kind of crumpled up, and his head looked sort of smashed, like a Halloween pumpkin."

I finally glanced at Raymond to see how he was taking this. I expected to see his familiar sneer. What I saw instead looked almost like pity. Something snapped inside me.

"That's it, you jerk," I said. God, I hated Raymond at that moment.

Raymond's mouth twitched. "Don't you get it, birdbrain? Don't you know who he was?"

Maybe it was the bird reference. I don't know. But I had my hands around his throat before he could get out another word. Raymond squirmed, red-faced, his hands gripping my wrists. Then Kyle was prying back my arms and yelling, "Look, Garson! Look behind you!" He spun me around and thrust out his chin, as if to point with it. "Over there. On Orville's head."

And there was Baby. Perched uncertainly on the top of Orville's head, the brown bird lifted one taloned leg and then the other experimentally. Then her wings bulged forward and spread, and she swooped across the room to a windowsill, landed and folded her wings to her body.

"*Told* you," said Raymond. He rubbed his neck.

Everyone stared, mesmerized, at the sparrow. All at once I felt my anger drain away. Raymond whistled low, a little trill, and Baby's wings shuddered.

"Averell wanted to watch her fly out that window," I said. "He didn't even know it won't open. He couldn't see the simplest things, sometimes."

"You should talk," said Raymond. He picked up the hammer lying in front of Justice Justice. Without ceremony he walked over to the window. Alarmed, Baby half-hopped, half-flew, to an armchair in the next corner. Raymond raised the hammer and swung at the windowpane, averting his face at the last second. The glass shattered magnificently, shards flying, raining on Raymond's shoulder. Baby was in flight again, in quick swoops, swerving just short of smashing into the walls. We all crouched instinctively, ducking or covering our heads. Finally, she alighted on the windowsill again, surrounded by glinting glass. She gave a few hops.

"Go for it," said Raymond.

Baby spread her wings then, flapped twice and soared through the jagged hole. We watched her fly over the trees and drop out of sight, over the lagoon.

After a minute, I broke the spell cast by Baby's flight to freedom. "Why'd you bring up my grandfather, Raymond?"

He didn't even look at me. Instead he stared at the empty sky where Baby had vanished from sight. "Never mind, Garson."

* * *

It's been at least a month since I wrote in this journal, but to tell the truth, not a whole lot has happened since Averell died and Baby escaped. Mostly, I've been too tired to do much. I don't know where all my energy goes.

Today I ducked down to the lobby to say goodbye to Raymond. They actually let him go home. Since the night of our trial, Raymond has transformed himself, like a butterfly in reverse, losing color and flightiness. Come to think of it, the change started even before the trial, right after Averell died. I remember Raymond sitting in the witness chair looking strangely normal. And the day after, I noticed that he'd clipped his nails, blunt like a guy's should be. Then he showed up in the day room with his hair cut short, no more bleached curls. After that the other quirks dropped one by one, like old petals. He started wearing button down shirts and shoes that laced. Sometimes he'd pass the whole day with stubble on his chin. But it was more than that; his voice got huskier, his gestures less showy. Pretty soon it was obvious to everyone: Madonna had left the building.

This morning I overslept again. Kyle told me Raymond had stopped by my room but didn't want to wake me. As I pulled on my pants, Kyle said there was a Cadillac on the front drive. So I dodged through a disabled fire exit and down the iron steps to the first floor. When the hall was clear, I slid along the wall to the lobby and peered around the corner. There was Raymond, standing in a cluster with his parents, head bowed and hands plunged deep into his front pants pockets.

Raymond's father was pudgy and mostly bald. He talked to Raymond's mother in the same tone of voice people use to scold a puppy for peeing on the carpet. "Can't you see where it says 'spouse?'" he said, shaking a hospital form in her face like a rolled up newspaper. She hovered, smiled meekly, one eyelid twitching. "Oh, Harry," she said, "I can't do *anything* right!" Snorting, Raymond's father bent over a nearby table and drew a determined line through his wife's signature. He signed his own name with a flourish, like it was the Declaration of Independence or something. Then he handed the paper to his wife with a harsh sigh. She hesitated before signing her own name, this time in the proper place, while Harry turned to Raymond.

"For God's sake, tuck in your shirt," he said.

Raymond began pushing his shirttails into his pants, turning slightly away from his father in the process. Then he looked up and saw me, half hidden around the corner, watching him. I kept a straight face but there must have been something there, because Raymond shrugged his shoulders and smiled wryly at me. By the time I raised my hand Raymond had turned to face his father again. They left moments later, Raymond's father leading the way, his mother straggling in the rear, and Raymond in the middle with hunched shoulders.

I hope he saw me wave. It's the closest we came to saying goodbye.

Back upstairs I wandered over to the janitor's closet to find Clarence. He was settled in the armchair, an open book resting on one meaty knee. He glanced up when I came in though, like he didn't mind being interrupted.

"Raymond get off okay?"

"Yeah," I said, "but his father was giving him a hard time."

"Some men have no business being fathers," he said, offhand, probably thinking of Marcel.

"Tell me about it," I said.

Clarence cocked his head to one side. "You tell me."

And then, just like that, I couldn't breathe. I tried to suck in air but my throat was closed. I gasped, gasped again and touched my neck. Clarence rose quickly from his chair and pawed through the closet shelves until he found a paper bag. He held the bag to my face, sort of frantic, like a man trying to defuse a bomb after setting the timer.

Ever since that day at the gas station I've had this sensation, like I'm one of those racehorses at the track, standing rigid in my stall with blinders on when the gun goes off and my gate flies open. Except that tiny moment, before I bolt out, just goes on and on, for an eternity, and I'm stuck there, paralyzed, unable to move forward. And then Clarence says "you tell me" and it's like the crop snapping down on my hindquarters, forcing my legs to push off, spurring me on, through the gate. But I'm not ready, the glare of the sun is too much, and my legs are weak, and I'm scared to run.

"Let's go find Dr. Fielgud," said Clarence.

"Okay," I said, inside the bag.

And we did.

Clarence left me alone with the doctor. I clutched the crumpled bag, but after a while my breathing was better so I didn't need it anymore. And then, for once, I did the talking, all about my father, until the glare dimmed and the hooves pounded down the track, mane whipping, running flat out, for the sheer exhilaration of it.

It's weird in a way. I spent my whole life trying to find out who my father was, but I had to kill him to do it.

Mom is visiting tomorrow. I'm really looking forward to seeing her again.

ROTTEN EGGS

TODAY I'M STUCK AT THE candling station. Row after row of glowing eggs chug by on the conveyor. Below the belt potent lamps shoot light through the shells to expose the eggs' innards. I should be checking for shell cracks and Rots but instead I'm watching Dolores at the next station.

Five weeks ago Dolores was standing where I am now, watching the eggs bounce along, when she turned pale, hunched over the conveyor and tossed her cookies. The second shift supervisor killed the engine, and the rest of us picked out three-dozen vomit-spattered eggs, our noses pinched, gagging at the stench. We spent an hour or so scrubbing the contraption before we could go back on line. Dolores was reassigned to take Haugh measurements at a station she can barf on without slowing production.

Something is wrong. I can't hear it over the machinery but I can tell that Dolores is humming by the way her lips press together, the soft flesh under her chin bulging like a bullfrog. There's no accounting for her cheerfulness, even on a Friday. A twisted red bandanna holds back most of her frizzy hair as she squints at the meter straddling a puddle of raw egg. Dolores glances up from her counter and catches me staring. When she smirks the light flashes off her silver braces. But the plucked arch of her eyebrow says *get back to work*.

Feeling guilty, I refocus on the eggs to scan for Rots. Rotten eggs come in many forms but they're all disgusting. Your Black Rots are some of the worst. Lit from below, the yolk looks purplish black, and if by some lousy luck the shell breaks, the stink is putrid, like road kill spiced with sulfur. Clone Rots have double yolks. Blood Rots are filled with violent, unappetizing bursts of red. Then there's the dreaded Mag Rots, crawling with tiny, wiggly maggots, inside and out. As I watch for the Rots, a cracked shell appears on the conveyor. I lean over to push the button beside the egg; it slides away to join the other eggs that can't be sold as First Quality, to the obscurity of a mayonnaise jar in Brunei or some such place.

I feel bad for all these eggs, cheated of their birthright as future chickens. Watching them reminds me of a movie I saw once about the last emperor of China. Squinting, I imagine that I'm high on a balcony in the Forbidden City, looking down on all the bald heads of banished eunuchs as they march toward the gates, each holding his balls in a jar before him. Like my imaginary eunuchs, the eggs strike me as sterile, emasculated, alone. I made the mistake once of trying to explain this to Dolores. She snorted and called me a city boy. "Every egg on this line means one less chicken," she said, "and believe you me, that's a good thing." She grew up in Black Earth, an hour from here down Highway C, in a tumbledown house with three bedrooms, nine siblings and no indoor plumbing. Chickens ran loose everywhere, even inside the house. "They're disgusting creatures," Dolores told me, wrinkling her nose. "They eat their own droppings."

Dolores couldn't wait to escape Black Earth. She dropped out of high school her senior year, intent on hitchhiking to New York. Her dream is to sing on Broadway. She made it 50 miles, to Mazomanie, before realizing she needed to save some money and straighten her crooked teeth first. Farm Fresh Eggs had a halfway decent dental plan and a string of trailers for employees to rent cheap.

I fell in love with Dolores the first time she came back to my trailer. She looked around the kitchen, hands on hips, and said, "You need some curtains in this dump." And just like that, the dull ache I'd felt since I left Milwaukee melted away, replaced by one of those rare and fleeting stabs of pure joy that no drug on Earth can produce.

For months I pestered Dolores to move in with me, give up her trailer and share mine. After I pointed out how much she'd save on rent, money she could use for New York instead, she finally agreed. Once she settled in my trailer and hung some bright curtains she found at K-Mart, I started proposing – first in the kitchen, then in my truck at stop signs, the frozen food section of the grocery store, even the break room at Farm Fresh Eggs. She was concerned that marriage might interfere with her singing career. I wasn't worried though. By then, I'd heard her sing.

After she upchucked on the eggs, Dolores went to the doctor. One week later we were married.

***

Riding home in the truck, Dolores hums *Blue Moon* as she taps her knee with one gnawed nail. Then she stops humming, twists in her seat and lays one hand on my forearm. "I've got some great news," she says.

"What's that?" I ask, my shoulders stiffening.

"An agent," she says, "is coming to hear me sing." She utters the word *agent* like a sinner might whisper *my Lord and Savior.*

"No kidding." The road beyond my windshield blurs. *What kind of agent trolls for talent in Mazomanie, Wisconsin?* In a rush, Dolores explains that the agent is Frank's cousin, in town for a visit. Frank Calderone bartends at the Mazomanie Supper Club where I've watched him watch Dolores sing. I've seen him gawk when she throws back her head under the spotlight, deep shadows in her collarbones and cleavage.

The truck hits a pothole and the glove compartment door springs open. Dolores slams it shut with a practiced air, but a bit more force than necessary. She expels a sigh. "What's wrong, Nick?"

"Nothing." I try to sound supportive. "An agent. That's great."

"You don't seem very enthusiastic."

"Well, the timing is awkward, that's all." I glance over at her. Her arms are crossed against her belly and her lips are pursed. Irritation tightens my jaw. "You forgot your seatbelt again, Dolores." She hesitates a moment before yanking the belt over her shoulder and securing it with a savage snap. Then she crosses her arms again.

"You can't always time everything just right," she says. We ponder that bit of wisdom in silence, but I don't think we're talking about the agent anymore.

***

My father died when I was eight and my mom never remarried. I always worried that she was lonely but that didn't stop me from making her miserable. We fought constantly, every time I came home with bloodshot eyes, or a note of suspension from my school, or riding in the back of a police cruiser. On the night of my high school graduation, I skipped the ceremony to relax on a sagging couch in our basement with a joint and a fifth of Jack Daniels. My mom came down in her housecoat and ordered me to leave. I don't remember the rest too well, but my sister insists that I went berserk, and smashed an ashtray against one wall, spewing ashes and crumpled butts and blue ceramic splinters everywhere. Then, Mindy claims, I lunged at my mom, who scrambled back up the stairs to the kitchen. What I do remember is Mindy, when she touched my arm, and told me that Mom had called the police. My little sister begged me to leave so I wouldn't get in any more trouble. I sat there shaking for a while, stubborn in my rage, until I saw the blue and red lights strobing against the glass in the window well. Then I got the hell out of there. That's how I was kicked out of my house, with nothing but the clothes I was wearing and thirty-seven dollars that Mindy pressed into my hand. She must have taken it from Mom's purse, which was a very un-Mindy-like thing for her to do. Twelve years old and she understood the situation better than I did.

I hitchhiked to Wisconsin Dells, a campy resort town up north crowded with water slides and miniature golf courses, where I found a job washing dishes at a hotel. Half my paycheck was deducted for lodging; they housed me in a room so small that, standing on my bed, I could touch the ceiling and all four walls. When vacationers deserted the Dells that fall, the hotel fired me, and I went on the road again, crisscrossing the state, working jobs in an appliance warehouse, a sub shop, a car wash, even once – for three days – an animal shelter. These jobs were all menial work for minimum wage, but I learned something from each one. Things like don't take the extended warranty on an electrical appliance, never eat a submarine sandwich unless you've seen it made, and stuff a buck in the car wash tip box if you want your antennae to come through unscathed. As for the animal shelter – the only job I quit, rather than wait to be fired – the lesson there is harder to describe. All the animals that weren't claimed or adopted were put down. It slayed me the way the supposed saviors of these abandoned animals became their executioners. I guess what I learned is this: don't depend on the kindness of strangers if you're all alone in the world. Better yet, don't be all alone in the world, if you can help it.

A guy I met in Green Bay, where I worked for a while as a janitor, told me about Farm Fresh Eggs. Said they were always looking for new employees. "The pay's for shit but it's easy work." I asked him why he hadn't stayed there if it was so great. "Too boring," he admitted, passing back the joint. "You burn out fast. And it absolutely kills your appetite for eggs." I've never been all that high on eggs anyway, so when my janitor job abruptly ended, I headed for Mazomanie.

***

Dolores spent the morning hunched over the kitchen table, gluing plastic nails to her fingertips with painstaking concentration, her hair twisted in fat pink sponge rollers. Then she took the truck and our checkbook into town to prowl through the aisles of the resale shop. She returned flushed and happy, with a glittery red dress that looked slinky even on the hanger. Now she is standing behind the microphone, framed by the front window of the Mazomanie Supper Club, her red dress shimmering under the spotlight, her silver braces glinting between slashes of red lipstick. Strawberry blonde hair falls in frozen waves over her shoulders, tamed by the rollers and cemented by hair spray that filled our trailer with its choking mist. She's singing my favorite, *Blue Moon*, her long red nails curled around the mike. *You saw me standing aloooone, without a dream in my heaaart, without a love of my oooown.* Her thin, reedy voice is hard to hear over the clink of silverware and echoing chatter of supper club diners. She lets the last note of the song linger even as she bends over to press the off button on her tape player, silencing her piano accompanist before the next song on the tape can begin.

Dolores acknowledges the scattered applause of several diners with a broad smile and an awkward move that is half-bow, half-curtsey. She replaces the mike atop its stand and sashays over to the bar where Tony Calderone is nursing his fourth bourbon and water. I'm standing there too, leaning back on my elbows. But Dolores' gaze is fixed on Tony as she slides onto the empty stool between the agent and me. We fumble through the introductions, accept fresh drinks from Frank behind the bar, and at my suggestion, move to a booth nearby.

It turns out Tony is from Atlantic City. He books his clients as lounge acts in the hotels and casinos there.

"So what did you think?" Dolores asks the agent, cutting right to the chase.

Tony steeples his stubby fingers and taps them against his chin. He's wearing a black onyx ring on one pinky. "First off, you need a new name."

Dolores practically leaps off her bench. "I have one!" she cries. She raises her hands on either side of her face, fanning her red-tipped fingers. "Dominique Del Ray." I wince inwardly, having tried my best to dampen her enthusiasm for that particular stage name.

Tony purses his lips and nods. "Not bad." Dolores elbows me under the table to say I-told-you-so.

"What about my act?" Dolores asks, her cheeks flushed.

117

"Well," Tony says, "you've got a certain presence, I'll give you that." He stirs his drink with one index finger. "'Course, you'd need to hook up with a real musician, someone to play the piano on stage."

"I can do that," Dolores says, leaning forward. A lock of her stiff hair sweeps a few inches across the tabletop, gathering crumbs, but she doesn't notice. "I can do whatever it takes."

I'm giving Tony the evil eye, which he is ignoring. "Just who," I say, "do you represent, exactly?"

Tony squints at me. "Mel Torme, ever heard of him?"

"Yeah," I say, real slow.

"His backup sax player from the old days, Paulie Pitula. I represent Paulie. He still plays the clubs." Tony twists his pinky ring reflectively. "There's a lot of the old greats playing Atlantic City these days."

"So your clients," I say – just by way of summary – "are a bunch of washed-up has-beens, and Atlantic City is a good place to *end* a career." A sharp pain flares just above my knee, where Dolores is squeezing my leg so hard I can feel her nails through my jeans.

"Don't mind him," Dolores says brightly. "Nick's a hopeless homebody. Stuck-in-the-mud of Mazomanie." She releases my knee and pulls her hand back to the tabletop, interlacing her fingers. One of her red nails has snapped off, on the finger with her wedding ring. She talks to Tony and flutters the ends her interlocked fingers. I see his eye wander to the nail that is stunted and peeling, surrounded by all the phony red ones.

Dolores doesn't notice the missing nail until we get back to the trailer. I convince her that it must have fallen off when she opened the truck door, after we left Tony at the Club. I figure that's the least I can do.

***

It's Sunday afternoon. Dolores is wearing a pair of jeans that have grown too tight. She bends over to root around for more food coloring in the lower cabinet, and I stare with guilty pleasure at a bottom so generous it would make Rueben blush. She has what my mother calls childbearing hips. Dolores is ambivalent about her curves. "These," she said once, slapping her thighs, "are the reason God invented liposuction." She takes my fondness for her figure as proof that I have no vision.

We're dying Easter eggs because it's Easter and the eggs were free. Dolores thinks they'll look pretty in a straw basket on the kitchen table. I'm trying to encourage this rare stab at homemaking on her part. I'm also trying to distract her from the silent phone.

"He wouldn't call on a Sunday anyway," Dolores says, "would he?"

"No," I say, "and it's a holiday, too, remember. He's probably at church or something." Tony Calderone attending mass is hard to imagine, but we both try. Our telephone has rung exactly twice in the week since we left Tony at the Mazomanie Supper Club. Dolores jumped to answer both times. She was snappy with her mother, but the telemarketer didn't fare as well. Dolores tore the poor slob a new one before she hung up.

It's quiet and stuffy in the trailer. There's no breeze today; the flowered curtains over the sink hang limp. Following Dolores' orders, I glue silver star-shaped sequins on an egg dyed baby blue while she stands before the stove to hard-boil a second bowlful of eggs. I hum under my breath – Sonny and Cher's *I've Got You Babe* – but stop when Dolores heaves a harsh sigh. In profile, her stomach has swelled. I look away and focus on my star-spangled egg, only to realize that I'm humming again.

"When Tony calls," Dolores says sharply, "just give the phone to me. I don't want you talking to him."

"Why not?" I put down my egg too hard and the shell crackles.

"I just don't." Dolores is staring down into a pot of water wafting steam, waiting impatiently for bubbles to appear. "You goad him on purpose."

My jaw tightens but I say nothing for a moment. What's the use of fighting about a phone call that will never come? Still, I don't want her blaming me. "All I did was ask him a few questions," I say in my own defense. "Besides, in a few months you're going to have your hands full." In the silence that follows I start to daydream, and smile at the image of my wife nursing my baby.

A hurtled egg cracks against my forehead. Egg white and yolk drip down my nose and spatter my cheeks and eyelids. Bits of shell drop onto my shirt, land in my lap. I use both hands to wipe my eyes.

"You never wanted me to sing!" Dolores yells. "You sabotage my career every chance you get!"

"I'm just trying to be realistic," I say quietly, shaking my gooey fingers. "We're starting a family here."

Dolores reaches into the bowl for another egg, cranks back her arm for another pitch. I raise my arms by reflex.

The telephone rings. We both freeze. Another ring shatters the stillness of our trailer. The egg falls from Dolores' hand, splats on the linoleum as she dives for the phone.

"Hello?" Her lips pull back to expose her braces. "Happy Easter to you, too!" She grips the receiver with both hands, her knuckles whitening. "Really?" She finally looks at me, her expression so joyful that my heart sinks into my stomach. "When?" With a sense of utter defeat, I realize that my wife has never looked more beautiful than she does at this moment.

Then, miraculously, her brow wrinkles. "What's that mean? For free? You're saying they're not going to pay me?" She leans against the counter for support. "Listen here, Tony," she says, like she's interrupting him, "I get all the *exposure* I need at the Supper Club." She listens some more, looking crestfallen. A blush appears on her face and spreads, staining her cheeks like the eggs we dyed pink. "Oh yeah?" she yells into the receiver. "Well, you're a crappy excuse for an agent!" She slams the receiver down into its cradle. Picks up the entire phone and hurls it across the trailer, ripping the phone cord from its socket. The phone slams into the wall with a small trill of the ringer, a crack of plastic, and clatters to the linoleum. Her knees caving, Dolores sinks slowly down to the floor, until her backbone presses against the cabinets under the counter. She buries her face in her kneecaps. Still dripping egg, I go to her and crouch at her side. Stroke her hair with my sticky fingers as her shoulders start to shake.

After a while, she raises her head, lets her knees drop to each side, and clutches her forearms to her stomach. A grimace of pain distorts her tear-streaked face.

"What's wrong?" I ask, frowning.

"Cramps," she manages to say. The crotch of her jeans is staining dark. The linoleum beneath her is splotched in red.

"Oh, Jesus," I say, "oh, no." I scramble for the phone to call 911 but there is no dial tone. Frantic, I try to reconnect the cord but the plug is just too damaged.

***

The eggs stream by but I'm watching Dolores. Finally she looks up, catches me staring, and gives me a wan smile. Now that her braces are off she has a beautiful smile, but sometimes I miss the cockeyed incisor, the front tooth gap, she had when we met. This new Dolores – subdued, her cheekbones sharp, clothes drab and nails natural, every day more elegant – is not the girl I married a year ago at City Hall. Not the girl who hung loud curtains in the kitchen of my trailer. Not even the girl who pelted me with chicken embryos.

Dolores cracks an egg on the counter with an unsentimental flick of her wrist. She looks up at me, her smile stern, and stabs her finger forward, pointing to the conveyor at my station. A Black Rot is jiggling by on the belt.

I reach down quickly to press the reject button and send the Black Rot tumbling down a chute. If Dolores were standing here instead of me, I know she'd do the same thing. She might even feel the same twinge of regret. She'd just feel it for reasons that are entirely her own . . . reasons I'd likely choose to ignore.

BORDER CROSSING

NADINE HASN'T SPOKEN TWO CIVIL words to me since we returned from Africa. I saw her yesterday at the beauty parlor, sitting under the domed dryer with her hair in pink curlers, paging through *House & Garden*, but her smile when she saw me was bleak, and her wave looked half-hearted. She didn't even tip up the dryer head to say hello. She just tossed aside her once-favorite magazine and picked up a *Newsweek* instead. I suppose she's disappointed that we went halfway around the globe to see gorillas, only to turn back at the border of Zaire. But that was her decision, not mine.

And it's not my fault the Italian lost his pants, either.

The whole trip was Nadine's idea. Not three months after she buried her stodgy husband, she saw a documentary on the Nature Channel about Dian Fossey cavorting with the gorillas, and suddenly Nadine was in a frenzy to go on safari. She pestered me about it for weeks, pressing brochures into my hands with pictures of gazelles leaping across the Serengeti, hippos yawning among the lily pads, and elephants raising their muddy, corrugated trunks. But the gorillas were what really caught her fancy. She was like a kid lobbying for a trip to Disneyland – a destination that truthfully I would have preferred. Africa sounded way too primitive for my liking, and I told Nadine as much. "I have no interest in eating wild game or sleeping in some old tent," I said. "What happens if I just want a hot dog?" Nadine argued that it was only for two weeks. "But I'll miss all my shows!" I countered. The inconveniences didn't seem to faze her, though. Maybe I was the only friend she had who could afford such a trip, because she just wouldn't let up on me. For weeks she wheedled and whined. So finally I said, sure Nadine, let's go. I'm not much for traveling, but that Nadine, she wore me down.

Ten days into our vacation, her enthusiasm hadn't flagged a bit. In Tanzania Nadine was captivated by the lions, elephants, zebras, hippos, giraffes, wildebeest and whatnot, the whole menagerie roaming that Ngorongoro Crater. At our tent camp in Uganda, Nadine found the crude accommodations charming. Finally, we were off to see the gorillas, the last adventure on our itinerary. Despite all the discomforts we endured, and by then we'd endured plenty, good ol' Nadine was still raring to go.

We were standing on the strip of sunbaked earth that divides Uganda from Zaire when Nadine had her change of heart.

***

Kintu, our broad-faced Ugandan guide, left us at his side of the border, saying our Zairian guide would find us on the other side. So we carried our own overnight bags, and they banged against our legs as we trudged across the dusty, hard-packed earth toward a cluster of thatched huts in the distance. The soil was a reddish brown, the color of dried blood. It was the dry season, and every breeze carried the dust from the ground and smoke from the hills where the farmers burned their fields. I wore my glasses all the time, and my floppy hat with the yellow daisies, but still my eyes were gritty and sore. Nadine plodded alongside me in silence.

"Why so quiet, Nadine?" I finally asked. "Was Kintu talking your ear off again?" In the jeep on the drive from the tent camp to the border, Nadine had ridden in front with Kintu. I watched him gesture and point, while Nadine listened and frowned, but from where I sat, bouncing in the back, the growling engine had drowned out their voices. In our short acquaintance with Kintu, he'd regaled us with stories of that old dictator Idi Amin, which if true, were enough to turn your hair white.

"Oh, Mavis," Nadine said, stopping abruptly, "why did we come to this god-forsaken place?"

"To see the gorillas." Perplexed by her outburst, but glad for the chance to rest, I set down my suitcase. "What's the matter with you, Nadine?"

The sun beat through the hot, hazy air. The thatched huts were closer now. I could see the guards standing outside in camouflage uniforms with big ugly guns slung over their shoulders.

"Kintu," Nadine sputtered, "says the most upsetting things about Zaire."

"Like what?"

"Like the banks are all failing, and the money is worthless, and the soldiers aren't even paid anymore." Nadine raised her hand to show me a damp wad of currency she held in her palm. "He said we'll have to bribe our way across the border."

I wasn't too shocked by this revelation. An hour earlier we'd stopped at a one-pump gas station and I'd watched Kintu negotiate for black-market gasoline. After a furtive glance at us, the scrawny attendant used a funnel to pour fuel from a bucket into our jeep's tank. As we drove away, Kintu admitted the gas was siphoned from tankers waylaid at the borders overnight. *How can you buy from thieves?* I asked, but he just shrugged. *If it weren't for the black market*, he said, *no one could buy anything.* And looking around, it was easy enough to believe, if not condone. Almost all of the locals traveled by foot, the women balancing tall bundles of plantains on their heads, the men clutching those awful machetes. A few lucky souls pedaled old bicycles standing up, often with something like a chair or mattress strapped to their backs. Between villages, a small truck would occasionally bear down on us, crowding our jeep to the side of the road and raising a huge cloud of dust as it passed. So despite the heat, we were forced to roll up our windows for several minutes whenever we saw an approaching truck. It was miserable, waiting in the stifling air for the dust to settle outside. But next to the locals walking along the road, we were sitting in the lap of luxury. I started wondering about those women in their vivid clothes. The bright colors of their wrapped skirts and headscarves looked so cheerful.

If I had to live in such poverty, I thought, I'd wear gray all the time, or maybe just fall on my machete and be done with it. But I know this much: I wouldn't steal or cheat or extort money from innocent tourists. No sir-ree. I glanced at the fold of bills in Nadine's outstretched hand. The nerve of these people, honestly! Stooping to something so crude as a bribe.

"Do what you want, Nadine," I said, "but I may just give those guards a piece of my mind."

Nadine darted a frantic glance at the guards in the near distance. "It's worse than that," she whispered.

"What's worse?"

"Kintu said the soldiers in Zaire, they . . ." and here Nadine faltered. Pink blotches appeared high on her pale pudgy cheeks.

"Spit it out, Nadine." My shoulder ached already and it was only noon.

"He said the soldiers will take money from the men, but they sometimes take the women . . . by force."

I snorted. "Don't be ridiculous, Nadine. We're Americans. Tourists. They wouldn't dare." I picked up my suitcase. "C'mon."

We started walking again, Nadine straggling a little behind. Pretty soon I could make out the guards' faces, like shiny chestnuts in the glaring sunlight.

"Remember the river?" Nadine asked. "The one we drove by on the way here?"

"What about it?" I faintly recalled the muddy flow of water between the acacia trees.

"Kintu said the bodies, the dead bodies, floated down that river from Rwanda for months. They were hacked by machetes. Kintu helped drag them from the river and bury them." Nadine seemed to shiver despite the heat. "He said they didn't eat fish from the river for a year."

"You mean the same river they washed our clothes in yesterday?" My skin was already starting to itch.

"I guess," Nadine said morosely.

After that we were quiet until we reached the first hut.

We stepped inside, out of the glare. The interior was so cramped and dim, we almost bumped into a couple that stood by the guard's table. They looked to be man and wife, both small and trim and dark-haired. They were talking low with their heads tipped together as the tall, muscled guard looked on. Our eyes still adjusting, Nadine and I dug in our fanny packs and handed the guard our passports and immunization cards. He didn't even smile or say hello, he was that rude, so I sighed several times, hands on hips, while he checked our papers. Midway through, he unhooked his gun from his shoulder and dropped it on a dusty old table. The barrel was pointed straight at Nadine, and for a split-second I thought she might scream. Her hand – the one holding the wadded bills – was twitching near the bulge of her khaki-covered thigh.

While we waited, I turned to the couple beside us. "Mavis," I said, sticking out my hand. The man's hand was warm but weak; the woman's was worse, damp and boneless. I swear, no one knows how to shake hands like an American.

To my surprise, they didn't even give me their names. "We may turn around," the man whispered.

"Where you folks from?" I asked the wife. "Italy," she said. Quite the conversationalists, those two.

"No luggage?" I asked. My arm ached. "In Uganda," said the man. "We had planned on a day trip." He squinted at the glare through the hut's entryway. "Now, I'm not sure."

It took forever, but the guard finally stamped our passports and motioned us toward the next hut. The Italian couple followed us with grim faces. In front of the hut, three guards were talking gibberish. That's when I noticed how young they were. Almost boys, really, except for their eyes. Their eyes looked lifeless to me. It occurred to me then, for some odd reason, that I'd yet to see an African with gray hair.

An unsmiling guard pointed to the counter, built into the wall of the hut, so we laid our suitcases there. He wasted no time in opening my Samsonite and pawing through the contents. He fiddled with my makeup case and scrutinized my girdle. Then he held up a flowered blouse I'd bought at K-mart especially for the trip. After a second he laid it on the counter and started to close my suitcase. Well, that did it for me. I may be a generous soul, when it comes to crippled kids and whatnot, but I wasn't about to donate my blouse to his girlfriend. No sir-ree.

"Not so fast, mister," I warned him, and snatched the blouse from the counter. I heard a little gasp behind me. I think it came from the Italian lady. The guard looked startled, then he tried to grab my wrist.

That's when Nadine made her move. She thrust her fist forward and uncurled her fingers. The guard didn't hesitate to scrape the bills from Nadine's palm. After counting the currency, he stood there for a moment, eyeing the four of us.

"We're turning back," the Italian man said to me in a low voice.

"We'll go with you," said Nadine, her eyes blinking rapidly.

The guard pointed to the Italian man. "Give me your pants," he said. Just like that.

"No," said the Italian, his jaw muscle bulging. "I need my pants." His wife's hand flew up to clutch his rigid arm.

"Give me your pants," repeated the guard, more sternly. The Italian shook his head. So what did the guard do, but reach across the counter and grab hold of my flowered blouse again.

By this time I was livid. I held on to that blouse with all ten fingers, arthritis be damned, while the guard tugged from behind the counter. Another guard peered around the side of the hut and smirked. But the thieving one wrinkled his forehead and narrowed his bloodshot eyes. Just when I thought the blouse might rip, he let go, and I staggered back a step or two. Then he picked up his gun, slung it over his shoulder. Walked around the counter, took my arm and said, "Come."

Next thing I know, Nadine is crumpled in a pile on the ground. Fainted dead away. The guard ignored her and pulled just above my elbow. His grip was strong and it hurt.

"Wait a minute," said the Italian man. "Just wait a minute, now." He glanced at me, then back at the guard. "Let her be," he said, sort of slow and deliberate, "and I'll give you my pants."

The guard didn't let go of me right away. He waited until the Italian had unbelted and unzipped his trousers, pulled them off over his shoes, and held them out to the brute.

***

We all trudged back across the red dusty field toward Uganda. Nadine was still shaky, her cheek smudged with dirt. The Italian man was walking in his boxer shorts and wouldn't meet our eyes, but his wife spoke a little in short, clipped English. She said they had traveled all over Africa, but they'd never seen anything like that border crossing. That was about all I could pry out of her, though. She seemed a little snooty, if you want to know the truth.

We found Kintu at a decrepit motel on the Uganda side of the border. He seemed surprised, and maybe even a little relieved, to see us. Nadine explained to him our change of plans, describing our "altercation" at the border, but she left out the most important aspects. Like she didn't even *mention* my flowered blouse. Thinking he had two days to kill before our return, Kintu had lent his jeep to another driver for the tour company, so he scrambled to find another vehicle. The replacement jeep, though, was a sorry excuse for transportation. The axel was wired to the chassis and the windshield was cracked like a spider web around what looked like a bullet hole. Naturally the jeep was covered with dust, inside and out. "You're joking, right?" I asked Kintu, but he just gave me his all-purpose shrug. I swear, these people are such defeatists.

The coup de grace came in a tiny village about halfway back to the tent camp. The road was so crowded by local pedestrians that Kintu was forced to stop the jeep for a swarm of children playing in the dirt. The engine promptly died, and we all got out to take a look under the hood. A little girl in a soiled pink dress – she couldn't have been more than five years old – took one look at me, pointed her little finger straight up at my face, opened her mouth as wide as it would go, and shrieked. Now, I realized I wasn't looking my best, but really! Kintu just smiled and said: "You're the first white person she's ever seen." I didn't say what I was thinking then, but rude is rude, even in a five-year-old. Anyhow, we couldn't get the jeep started without a push from the ragtag horde of smelly locals who had gathered around us, so we climbed back in the jeep and let them push while Kintu popped the clutch. When the jeep started and the pushers fell back, Nadine turned to wave her thanks like they'd done us some big fat favor. I couldn't see that they had anything better to do. And there was no excuse for this broken down jalopy from the tour company. So I leaned forward and hissed my verdict in her ear: "Nadine, this is just *unacceptable* service." She gave me the strangest look, then, like I'd just passed gas in public or committed some other grievous crime against humanity.

For the rest of the ride, I closed my sore eyelids so I wouldn't have to see the depressing scenery flit by my window. All those mud hovels and abandoned-looking children and the occasional waterhole choked with dusty people, washing and bathing and drinking from the same place. No wonder Ebola is such a worry here, not to mention the malarial mosquitoes and the AIDs-infected monkeys and God knows what other forms of pestilence. It all reminded me of a trip I took once to Cancun, back when my Albert was still alive. We made the mistake of renting a car and driving outside the resort area. It was dreadful, the squalor those Mexicans live in. I for one refuse to pay for the privilege of being depressed, so we turned around and hightailed it back to the resort. The Americana Cancun was one of those all-inclusive places, and very pleasant if you overlooked the half-nude sunbathers.

By some miracle we managed to make it back to the camp in one piece. There, Nadine and I spent three more nights lying in our tent, listening to termites munch the bamboo and hippos moan near the river. Kintu warned us hippos kill more people than any other wild animal, so we should never get between a hippo and water. As if I'd go anywhere near that filthy river. For our last dinner at the camp, the waiter served us tilapia, but he hadn't bothered to remove the fish heads, much less the bones. Between Kintu's tall tales of floating bodies and those beady eyes staring up from my plate, I couldn't touch my meal.

The next day Kintu drove us to Nairobi, where we caught our first flight to London, then on to New York, Chicago, and finally, home sweet home.

I've recovered from the whole ordeal, but Nadine is another story. Within days of our return, she'd resigned her membership in the Garden Club, claiming she was too busy to attend the weekly lunches or serve on the

GardenFest committee this year. Rumor has it that she's joined Amnesty International. The local group, I've been told, is this motley crew of old hippies and college radicals who meet in a drafty church basement to write letters to Fidel Castro and such. Like that's going to do any good. Do they really think that the likes of Mobutu, the character who's ruled Zaire for thirty-odd years, is going to give a darn about their outrage? I suspect that Nadine's feeling sorry for those poor Africans, despite the conniving ways she witnessed firsthand.

I also get the distinct impression that Nadine blames *me* for the whole border-crossing fiasco. Which really fries my bacon. It wasn't *my* fault we missed the gorillas. As for the Italian, I think it's fair to say that he gave up his pants of his own free will.

But just try to tell that to Nadine.